I can't do this anymore....

Dear Erica, I wrote this out because I know I wouldn't be able to say what I need to say in person. I know I wouldn't make sense of any of it. I don't deserve you—

Ted noticed that his fingers were shaking, and he crumpled the piece of paper into a spitball. Reaching into the pocket of his warm-up pants, he slid out his cell phone and scrolled through the PHONEBOOK.

"Hello, Theodore. I'm wildly disappointed to have missed you, but, alas, I've run off on another errand. If you'll be so kind as to leave the nature of your call, I will return it as soon as is humanly possible. Ciao." *Beep.*

A muscle twitch joggled the joints in Ted's hand, and he squeezed the phone to his ear. "I quit," he whispered. "I'm ending this, okay? Enough. I can't take this, and—I'll find a way to pay you back for the semester, and that's it, okay?"

Stabbing END, Ted shrugged his shoulder over his cheekbone and smeared the teardrops perched on his eyelids. He ripped the battery strip off the phone and propped his left leg on the corner of James's desk. Ted slipped his fingers through a handle of José Cuervo tequila and watched the golden water crash against the label. . . .

OTHER BOOKS YOU MAY ENJOY

JAKE COBURN

LoveSick

An Imprint of Penguin Group (USA) Inc.

Special thanks to Elaine Markson Literary Agency and my brilliant editor, Julie Strauss-Gabel

SPEAK

Published by the Penguin Group

Penguin Group (USA) Inc., 345 Hudson Street, New York, New York 10014, U.S.A.

Penguin Group (Canada), 90 Eglinton Avenue East, Suite 700,
Toronto, Ontario, Canada M4P 2Y3 (a division of Pearson Penguin Canada Inc.)

Penguin Books Ltd, 80 Strand, London WC2R 0RL, England

Penguin Ireland, 25 St Stephen's Green, Dublin 2, Ireland (a division of Penguin Books Ltd)

Penguin Group (Australia), 250 Camberwell Road, Camberwell, Victoria 3124, Australia
(a division of Pearson Australia Group Pty Ltd)

Penguin Books India Pvt Ltd, 11 Community Centre,
Panchsheel Park, New Delhi - 110 017, India

Penguin Group (NZ), 67 Apollo Drive, Mairangi Bay, Auckland 1311, New Zealand
(a division of Pearson New Zealand Ltd)

Penguin Books (South Africa) (Pty) Ltd, 24 Sturdee Avenue,
Rosebank, Johannesburg 2196, South Africa

Registered Offices: Penguin Books Ltd, 80 Strand, London WC2R 0RL, England

First published in the United States of America by Dutton Books,
a member of Penguin Group (USA) Inc., 2005
Published by Speak, an imprint of Penguin Group (USA) Inc., 2007

10 9 8 7

Copyright © Jake Coburn, 2005
All rights reserved

LIBRARY OF CONGRESS CONTROL NUMBER: 2005002140
ISBN: 0-525-47383-1 (hc)

Speak ISBN 978-0-14-240802-5

Printed in the United States of America

Photograph of woman's lips on page iii © LWA-Stephen Welstead/Corbis.

Love

Sick

Preface

I'm a slut for a good rumor. Two-timers. Welshed bets. Party brawls. I shut up and listen.

Last October, I'm halfway through a BLT when my friend starts rambling about this prep-school girl whose banker father paid all these people to spy on her—the works: e-mails, GPS, cell and credit-card records, kids in her dorm. Three months into the sting, she vanishes, and her father winds up in a Park Avenue hospital.

It takes me a week to find out her name, Erica Prakers, and another two to dig up an e-mail address. I still squirm every time I think about my stupid introductory message. Or maybe it's just her two-word reply: FUCK YOU. I send her three more e-mails, each a week apart and shorter than the last, but I never hear back. Then, two days into the New Year, EP231094@yahoo.com flashes onto my INBOX.

jake — i needed a few weeks to check up on you (hope you don't mind). i read your novel. some parts were funny but it got a little whiny (no offense). if you're really serious about this book idea you should email ted. it was his story before it was mine and we both need to agree to make it yours. anyway email me back at this yahoo address. had to change accounts. erica

Six months and three hundred and twenty-seven e-mails later, I'm sending Ted and Erica a first draft of their story. At times, it seems impossible that a shy two-guard from suburban Illinois had pocketed an envelope filled with fifteen hundred dollars or that a New York City debutante had stolen a car. But I'll let Ted and Erica explain themselves on the ink.

What follows is a nonfiction novel, or a fictional exposé, or maybe it's just a love story. In most instances, real names and places have been changed or deleted. Aside from the www.High-smith.com e-mails, the writing in *LoveSick* is almost entirely my own. The best lines, of course, are theirs.

Jake Coburn
NEW YORK CITY

 **AUGUST**

John leaned forward and set his Styrofoam cup in between the front legs of his folding chair. "John L., alcoholic."

"Hi, John," the room roared back.

"I'm excited to introduce tonight's speaker," John said, twirling his sober key chain around a finger. "When I first met him, I figured I'd spilled more than he'd drank. But he's one of us, and I just hope he knows it. And he's here tonight to share his experience, strength, and hope. So, without further, please help me welcome Ted Y."

The group applauded energetically and then shifted their plastic chairs to face Ted. He was wearing a Foot Locker sweatshirt and baggy blue warm-up pants with white pull-away buttons along the outer seams. Ted hadn't shaved his head since the varsity season ended, and his shaggy bangs were just beginning to droop over his fresh green eyes.

Ted slumped down in his chair. "Name's Ted. Alcoholic."

The circle echoed his name.

"And I guess some of you know my story already," he said,

surveying the group. Twenty-four eyes. Twelve AAs. Nine men. Three women. Two newcomers counting days from Crossroads Halfway House. John winked at him, and Ted tried to smile back.

"Ninety days without alcohol," Ted began again. "This is my first time qualifying, and I guess I don't really know where to start. . . ." Ted felt like he chose his words more carefully than almost every other AA he knew. In Paul's car, on the way to the meeting, he'd tried to rehearse. He'd even scripted a few anecdotes on an index card.

"At the beginning," John suggested.

The How It Works tradition was for all newcomers to tell their story on their three-month anniversary. Ted had spoken in meetings before but only when he'd been called on and only for a minute or two.

Ted filled his lungs and focused on the sober placards around the community center. EASY DOES IT sat above the glossy CPR poster, FIRST THINGS FIRST rested on the pre-K library shelves, and LET GO AND LET GOD balanced atop the cluttered announcements board.

"Well," Ted said, "I guess I've always been a drinker. Like, as a little kid, before I figured out the different kinds of booze, I used to steal sips from my father's glass. Maybe it's just a lot simpler to say I love the effects. I mean, for me, the first drink feels like someone flicked a light switch inside me or something. I'm just on."

Half the group nodded. Watching Paul rock back and forth helped ease Ted's grip on his chair. Of all the AAs in the room, Paul was the only one who drank exactly the way Ted did, completely alone.

"When I was in grade school, I was a pretty solid pitcher. Good for my age at least, and my father would always split a beer with me if I pitched a complete game or a bunch of shutout innings.

It sounds funny to say, but I started thinking about that drink up on the mound. Like whether I'd get a separate glass or the half-bottle," Ted finished, folding his voice into his chest.

"So I should probably skip ahead to my freshman year of high school. Which is when I started drinking at parties and stuff. And I guess my first couple parties were pretty basic. Making a scene, puking, fighting. Nothing real special to you guys."

Stephen lazily stretched his eyebrows. Ted instantly felt like flipping him off. A retired Air Force captain, Stephen hadn't touched a drop until his late thirties, and he loved to put his arm around Ted's shoulders and tell him how lucky he was to find Alcoholics Anonymous at the young age of seventeen.

"And then I had my first jackpot. I don't remember much about the evening, but I guess it started out after having one of my big nights behind the arc. We were in the state basketball quarters, and I'd drained five or six threes as a two-guard off the bench. Playing Holy Name, I think."

Shirley grinned and rested her palms gently on top of her Big Book. A squat pharmacist, Shirley had lost her license for stockpiling benzodiazepines in her attic. For the last two years of her sobriety, she'd been working as the editor of the *Courier*'s local sports column. When Ted had first started going to meetings, she'd pretended not to recognize the county's leading point scorer.

"So, and I guess there's no reason to beat around the bush on this, but I pissed myself at this house party. I'd passed out on the arm of some couch, and then, like three hours later, a couple of my friends dragged me into the shower. I definitely had a bunch of the shame that people here talk about. I mean my jeans were soaked through. But what stuck with me was the fact that I remembered sort of half-dreaming to myself, *I gotta fucking piss.*

And I swear, I was fucked up enough to actually think through the whole thing and say, *Fuck it, piss.*"

The circle burst into a jumble of laughter and applause, and Ted forced a smile. He knew every drunkalogue was expected to have a few laughs, and he'd decided he was terrible at straight jokes.

"Well, I guess I should jump ahead to when I started drinking at home. I think I realized that drinking at parties wasn't working for me, so I started buying bottles at McGeers and having a few after my folks went to sleep. I'd still go out on weekends, but I'd usually try and avoid the drink. Like at a party or whatever, I'd carry around a cup of orange juice and everybody figures I'm boozing it up. See, I knew that if I was going to start, I needed to do it in a real safe place. You know, so I didn't have to deal with everybody else and the bullshit."

"Yup." John grunted and rested his elbows on the back of his chair.

Ted wove his hands together and snapped his knuckles. His fingers had been broken and jammed so many times that only two of them still formed truly straight lines. The rest of his digits jutted off at slight angles. On the court, Ted used to call his crooked fingers "little lightning bolts."

"And after a couple months, I realized what my true calling was. As a drinker, I mean. I'd place a tape in my VCR before school, set it to record the best college game I could find in the guide, buy a bottle after practice, and then spend my midnight sipping and watching. Studying tape, drinking, nobody bothering nothing."

Ted adjusted his chair and instinctively flexed his right knee. The surgeon had said his sensitivity would go away after six to twelve months, but he wasn't sure he wanted it to. Paul claimed it was a daily reminder of why Ted shouldn't drink.

"And I guess things kind of just went from there through high school. I mean, most of my drinking took place on the floor of my bedroom, studying tape. My outsides didn't really change all that much. Like I was a B or B-minus student, and I pretty much stayed there, coasting. Friends were basically the same. My numbers on the floor actually got a lot better. I think I've always seen my drinking as like real alone time, for me to get free of all the bullshit. Other people aren't involved, but on purpose."

Ted noticed that one of the guys from Crossroads Halfway House was fiercely squeezing a tennis ball in his right hand. The first time Ted sat through How It Works, he spent the hour rolling a quarter back and forth across his knuckles. After the meeting, John had introduced himself, and Ted had asked him to sign his court attendance card. John had surveyed Ted's knee brace and purple-black shiner and then thanked him for stopping by.

"And then I started breaking my own rules. Things were going too well, I think, looking back. It was graduation, and I'd been accepted to this Ivy League school and given an under-the-table free ride. They even escorted me around the campus, introducing me to the coaching staff and players and treating me like some sort of star.

"So whatever, about three months ago, I'm sitting there on the floor of my bedroom, exactly as I always did. And I've finished off my bottle, and I'm sitting there dying for another couple drinks, knowing a couple is all I need to really finish off the evening and have a good sleep. To do the buzz right.

"And I decide to take a late-night spin over to McGeers. I figure I'm definitely sober enough to drive the mile, especially on roads that are probably empty anyway. So I'm on Fountain doing thirty-five, and I spot some sort of animal or something. Maybe it's a chipmunk or skunk, so I swerve to the right to dodge it.

Probably didn't even need to, but I did anyway. I hit the gravel cushion, and the wheel starts to stick, like I can't get the tires back on the road. I swerve back, hard, and the tires fly off the gravel. And that's it; a fifty-year-old maple wipes out the truck and my knee."

Ted reached for the cup of coffee that he'd forgotten about and wet his throat. He noticed his fingers were shaking, and he rested the cup back on the scuffed linoleum.

"I guess I was in the hospital for two days, had a bunch of surgeries, tubes and machines, the whole thing. Judge Hall didn't tag me with a DUI, but he gave me a court-meeting card and told me if I didn't go to AA meetings for ninety days, he'd throw the book at me. So I showed up here later that week."

Ted's eyes scrolled down the red lettering on the hanging shade that inscribed the Twelve Steps. On the ride over, Paul had said to concentrate on Step 1 and the words *powerless* and *unmanageable*.

"Well, so . . ." His voice trailed off. Ted knew the more people he told, the more true it would feel. "I guess I'd have to say that everything fell apart when I lost my ride. To college, I mean. About three weeks ago, my new coach calls me up and tells me they're giving my cushy scholarship to some center from Oklahoma. A month before I'm supposed to leave, and here I am with no financial aid, and no other schools accepting applications, and fuck me."

Ted flexed the taut muscles in his back and pulled off his Foot Locker sweatshirt. The yellowing armpits of his undershirt were stained from layers of deodorant and sweat. He felt a single salty droplet run a cool streak down his rib cage.

"So that pretty much brings me up-to-date. Working at Foot Locker for mini-wage, most of my friends gone for preseason. To be honest, I've spent the last week debating almost everything. The court card was done four days ago, and I feel like all I do is talk myself in circles. I mean, I still don't understand why I haven't had a drink yet. Before, I guess I didn't want to show up here hung over, but now I feel like . . .

"It's not that I don't think I belong here during meetings. It's just that outside of meetings I feel like I'm overreacting or something. Like none of the bad shit most of you guys talk about has really happened to me. Lost jobs, ex-wives, stealing. I don't know. I guess I've never felt so stuck in my life. Going fucking nowhere."

Date: Thursday, 14 Aug 18:19:21
From: MichaelFIN@Highsmith.com
To: CharlesFIN@Highsmith.com

Cheers,

Many apologies for these deliciously tacky pseudonyms. It appears there's no place less private than a Fortune 500 email system, as I'm sure you're well aware, so I've taken refuge in a rural portal. Highsmith Entertainment provides fifteen Arizona suburbs with high-speed cable service, and they're generous enough to offer a free 10MB mailbox to anyone willing to brave their antediluvian HTML. Not surprisingly, I strongly discourage you from clicking the *Save Username* and *Password* icon on your computer.

As you've likely guessed, I will also be communicating with our grantee through Highsmith. Email is surely the most private and convenient means available to a college freshman, and it will provide me with the option of forwarding you pertinent communiqués. I'm still reviewing the merits of a daily, weekly, or biweekly correspondence, and I should be interested in your thoughts on the matter.

Alternatively, perhaps we might reserve judgment until we've finally settled on a young grantee. I have two interviews scheduled tonight, and I am quite confident that one of these prospects will meet our highest standards. The Tourettic Kentuckian, while needy and handsome, was truly an aberration, and I continue to question a college admissions process that would fail to alert the committee of such a condition.

Finally, I am thrilled to write that we are agreed on a 25%-25%-50% split. As such, $75,000 is currently due and payable, $75,000 will be due October 1st, and $150,000 will be due December 1st. At your earliest convenience, please contact my lawyer on Grand Cayman. I have alerted him that you will be requiring his assistance.

Fondly,
Michael

Date: Thursday, 14 Aug 19:05:50
From: CharlesFIN@Highsmith.com
To: MichaelFIN@Highsmith.com

M — Glad we settled on split. Put in a call to your guy in the BWIs. Still waiting for my tax guy to run the nums. Sorry about the KY freak. Told Jack to double-check the medical forms. University

Chancellors are like fucking CEO's. No clue how to get anything done.—C

Erica turned the corner of Fifty-ninth and Third Avenue carrying a Medium Brown Bag filled with denim. Cycling through her cell phone's PHONEBOOK, she stabbed L CELL. The fizzy ringer stuttered into Laura's voice-mail bank.

"Blah, blah, blah," Erica sang, grinning. "Call me, babe."

She walked through the sliding glass doors of the Food Emporium and listened to the *pi-tang* of infrared checkout scanners. All around her, paper shopping bags were popping open and swallowing stacks of cans and cereal boxes, melons and cartons of juice. She rested the straps of her Medium Brown Bag in the crease of her elbow and picked up a plastic grocery basket. Stepping around an elderly man studying a handful of coupons, she walked toward aisle two.

Erica plugged in her iPod earbuds and scrolled through Ani DiFranco's first album. She'd been craving the chaotic string speed of "Both Hands" since she got off the subway. Last week she and Laura had spent half an hour discussing the lyrics and the way the violins seemed to introduce each chorus effortlessly.

Erica strolled across the checkered tiles past the bread racks and stopped in front of the rice-cake display. She picked up two bags of Quaker Butter Popped and then tossed one back. At thirty-five calories per cake, Quakers were the safest treat that wasn't celery or carrots. They tasted like cardboard soaked in margarine, but each cake was bigger than the palm of her hand.

Erica turned the corner into aisle three and paused in front of the Hostess rack. She'd been thinking Apple Fruit Pies all day, but the oil from the miniature pies had seeped through the green wrappers, and she wondered how long they'd been sitting on the shelf. Surveying the rack, she spotted a package of Powdered Donettes. The six Donettes were stacked firmly against each other, and the bleached confectioners' sugar revealed cracks and faults in the dough. At the bottom of the packaging, a drift of loose powder was spilling into the plastic seams.

Erica grabbed three six-packs of Donettes and quickly placed them in her grocery basket. Then she turned and started walking casually down the aisle. After a few steps, between olives and peanut butter, she jostled the forearm that was carrying the Medium Brown Bag. The twine handles spread apart across her skin and produced a shaded well. She stopped again in front of the canned bean section and assumed her contemplative shopper's pose.

Tapping her New Balances against the tiles, Erica scanned the aisle. Two middle-aged men were studying the back label of an Ortega salsa jar. She lifted her palm from her waist, plucked two six-packs of Donettes from her grocery basket, and dropped them into the Medium Brown Bag. The denim silently cushioned the weight of the Donettes, and she smiled at the shiver of adrenaline spiderwebbing down her back in four-four time. Erica had tried shoplifting cosmetics, clothing, and CDs, but nothing cleared her sinuses like supermarkets—the brighter the better. All the other shit was too boring not to just buy.

In aisle four, Erica found herself pretending to search for the Sun-Maid raisins, as if she didn't know exactly where they were. She wasn't sure why she was putting on a show, but it instantly annoyed her. She bent down on one knee and reached for a three-pack of lunchbox-sized containers. They were the perfect antidote to the dizzies, and they never left her feeling bloated or too full.

As she cradled the raisins in her hand, Erica suddenly realized that the Sun-Maid and Hostess logos were exactly the same: a bright yellow sun with a sharp-spiked circumference and a fire-engine-red backdrop. She instantly felt like ripping out her ear-buds and screaming, "Conspiracy!" The more she thought about it, the more obvious it seemed. Anybody who ate enough of those soggy buttons would eventually reach for true powdered satisfaction. The Sun-Maid lady could sit there with that glassy-eyed smile and bushel of grapes, but Erica knew she was Hostess's bitch.

She debated throwing the Sun-Maids back onto the shelf, but she'd already placed them next to her Quaker cakes. Besides, she needed to pay for a few things. Leaving a supermarket empty-handed was like walking out in your underwear.

Erica wandered slowly down the frozen-foods aisle, waiting for the conspiracy buzz to dissolve. Normally, when she was transferring items to a shopping bag, she liked to spread the process out. After the first drop, she'd ride her spiked pulse until she was craving it again. Sometimes she'd even play with her withdrawal, testing herself, seeing how long she could stand to wait. She usually finished up in aisle five. The freezers were always the safest aisles to work. The sealed glass doors were the perfect subterfuge, and the ambient hum absorbed any accidental clatter.

Erica rounded aisle five with the three packages of Powdered Donettes snuggled at the bottom of her Medium Brown Bag. The vibrating tickle of her cell phone broke her stride, and she uncorked her earbuds. The display flashed BIDNEZ.

"Hey, Dad," Erica muttered, flexing her wrist. The grocery basket still felt light as she turned into aisle six.

"Hey," Charles said excitedly. "Just wanted to sync up and make sure you got my message about Sotheby's tonight. I—"

"Yup."

"'Cause I only had one bar."

Erica eyed a glass jar of Del Monte Mandarin Oranges in light syrup. The peeled slices of fruit swam listlessly around the container like goldfish. "I got it. I was going to call you back."

"So you want to watch me buy this Henry Moore?"

"You're buying Henry Moore, Dad? I thought he was dead."

"Clever." Charles groaned. "It's the *Mother and Child*. Bronze. Should blow out the door at an even three hundred."

"Three hundred—?"

"Thousand," Charles finished.

"Right," Erica said, distracted, placing the Del Monte jar in the center of her basket. She pictured herself sitting at the kitchen table, studying the floating orange bodies.

"Or we could do dessert and coffee afterward. I know you're not wild about Susan's friends—"

"I can handle The Ferret." Erica had nicknamed her father's girlfriend The Ferret because she wrapped herself around Charles's neck and bit everybody else.

"Also, had a short call with Doctor Rudas. I assume he gave you the heads-up."

Erica laughed and searched the organic cereal rack. "He told you I'm cured, right?"

"Bottom line," Charles said, coughing, "he's still really against you going."

"Then you shouldn't have pulled all those strings to get me in."

"Erica, you got a fucking fifteen-seventy on the SATs and—"

"You know he reads his mail during our sessions."

"What?" Charles stammered.

"If I'm not talking, he starts opening his mail and paying bills."

"Erica, I know he's told you school's a mistake."

"Yeah," Erica said, watching a toddler paw at the bars of his shopping-cart high chair. "Something about a stable environment and medical supervision, right?"

"And you said?"

Erica shielded the receiver. "I told him his son was dealing Ecstasy at Collier."

"Fuck me," Charles cried.

"He is, you know," she declared. "It's a fact."

"Erica, why do you—"

"But he can attack me?" Erica said incredulously. "Besides, it's the truth."

"I don't believe this."

"Why isn't his kid relevant?" she continued. "It's relevant to me. I mean I'm the one who's supposed to take his advice seriously."

"We'll talk about this later."

"You don't want to hear where the conversation went from there?"

"Later, Erica."

"Ciao, Papa," Erica said, arriving at the front promenade of the Food Emporium. She recognized Bethany and Heidi at the express lanes, but she didn't feel like hustling through the line. She enjoyed waiting, stretching the high. Besides, she'd already decided she wanted to pay Kevin.

Kevin was working checkout counter 7. He always worked 7 or 2, and Erica had never had the courage to ask why. There were three women standing in Kevin's line, and Erica felt a flush of jealousy. No other line had more than two customers, and she hated the idea of being lumped in with other fans. If she shopped at the end of Kevin's late shift, she'd normally get to enjoy him all by herself. He'd always take a few extra seconds with her, examining her conscientious purchases while she carelessly flipped through *People* or *Redbook*. They'd never said more than "Hi" or "How's it going?" but she'd spent the summer dreaming their first date.

Erica inched forward in line, trying not to look annoyed. Kevin smiled as soon as he saw her, and she could suddenly feel how dull his job was, how refreshing her face must be. His toned forearms and sandy Hispanic complexion made her want to lean over the conveyor belt and kiss his polyester vest.

Erica handed Kevin the raisins and watched him slowly wave the packaging over the scanner. Passing him the Quaker cakes, she imagined herself sitting shotgun in Kevin's coupe. They're riding up the West Side Highway, hip-hop beat tickling the goose bumps on her chest, Kevin's hand carefully massaging the inside of her thigh. He's talking, not about summer homes or vacations or lacrosse tactics, and he's telling her how much he loves her body. She rolls her eyes as he starts to describe the riverbed of her lower back.

The bass of Kevin's voice pierced Erica's daydream. She had no idea what he'd just said.

"Pardon?" As soon as Erica opened her mouth, she was disgusted with herself. If she'd thought about it for a second, she would have chosen "Excuse me" or "Sorry" or just "What?"

Kevin pointed to the end of the cashier's counter. "Paper or plastic?"

Date: Thursday, 14 Aug 20:14:40
From: MichaelFIN@Highsmith.com
To: CharlesFIN@Highsmith.com

Cheers,

I'm afraid I must beg for another mulligan, though thankfully for reasons bearing little resemblance to our Louisville Slurrer. While Cori was exceptionally receptive to the concept of a scholarship program, she presented several glaring flaws. Foremost among Cori's defects was her exceedingly impressive intellect. As a classical pianist and oboist, she has spent the better part of her summer piecing together the rudiments of an 18-Tone method of composition. Naturally, I think it would be foolish to select such a precocious young woman. We're in the market for a fair and gentle soul, a docile constitution.

While I obviously had greater hopes for Cori, I am entirely convinced that my evening's final candidate possesses our requisite ingredients: attractive, moderately bright without a sparkle of inventiveness, and poorer than the dirt on a subway vagrant's bottom.

Lastly, our West Indian counselor has informed me that he is still awaiting your final signature. If you still have any lingering questions, please don't hesitate to include them in your response.

Fondly,
Michael

Date: Thursday, 14 Aug 20:34:56
From: CharlesFIN@Highsmith.com
To: MichaelFIN@Highsmith.com

M—Keep shopping. Kid just needs eyes and ears, tight mouth, common sense. Good luck with Tiny Tim. You can't afford to keep bogeying holes. Will deliver check when you deliver the kid. Given our puff sheet, my credit will hold me until the deal goes live. Enjoy the Drive-Thrus. You eating McD's, BK, Denny's???—C

"You sounded freaking good," Paul said, blowing on the filter of a menthol Basic. "Real freaking good."

Ted leaned his forehead against the passenger-side window of Paul's Subaru and watched the fleet of rain droplets shuddering on the glass.

"It was a solid meeting." Paul waved his match out. "Which is all you can ask for."

Ted lifted his eyebrows dismissively. "I can't remember what I said."

"Same thing happened to me at my six-monther," Paul said, exhaling.

Eight weeks ago, Paul had spotted Ted walking home from their Tuesday men's meeting, and he'd offered to start giving him rides. Ted didn't like owing people favors, but he'd junked his truck after the accident, and he hated asking his parents.

"You were honest," Paul declared. "I mean, I know from us talking that you told the truth, the whole truth, and nothing but the truth, so help you, Higher Power."

At first Ted had been convinced that Paul was a pedophile. He couldn't understand why a twenty-five-year-old engineering student would go out of his way to pick up a teenager he barely even knew. Then a week later, Paul spent the drive to Vision for You crying about how much he missed his ex-fiancée and the house he was still planning to build for them. And Ted realized Paul was willing to do just about anything to stay sober, even pick up some kid who lived ten miles away.

Ted sat back and adjusted his warm-up pants. "I felt like everybody was judging me."

Paul turned onto Sheldon Street, hanging five miles below the speed limit. "I wouldn't let that eat at you. Nobody thinks about anybody but themselves."

"Maybe you're right."

"So, you hit your knees before you spoke?"

"I think I said the Serenity Prayer—"

"That's prayer, all right. You turned it over."

"I guess," Ted agreed.

"Higher Power doing for us what we can't do for ourselves."

At ninety-four days sober, Ted's Higher Power was his official NBA game ball. Paul and John had told him that he needed to pick something bigger than a lightbulb and not himself, and he'd chosen Spalding's finest product. Selected grain genuine leather. Eight deep channels filled with nine pounds of pressure. Commissioner's signature across the front. Ted hated the idea of bowing before some graying old man, so he chose a Higher Power he could hold.

"So we're doing Back to Basics tomorrow?" Paul asked.

"Why not." Ted crossed his right leg and massaged his knee, tracing the buried metal.

Paul nodded through a plume as he turned onto Lasker Street and pulled up to a horseshoe Colonial.

Ted reached to shake. "Later."

"Quick spot check," Paul announced. The engine sent a metallic clang down Lasker Street.

"Come on."

"It's the price of the ride," Paul insisted.

Ted flashed him a stop sign. "Went to a meeting. Spoke to three other alcoholics," he said, folding his thumb and index finger into his palm. "Prayed." Ted dropped his middle finger. "Read two pages of the Big Book," he continued, curling his ring finger into a fist.

Paul smiled and wiggled his pinkie. "Daily gratitude list."

"I'll write it."

"No time like the present." Paul reached up to his sun visor and plucked out a black Bic. "I'll wait."

Ted shook his head and dug a Starbucks napkin out of the cup holder. "Yeah."

"Shouldn't take more than thirty secs—"

"Yeah," Ted interrupted. "Sobriety, my health, my parents' health. One, two, three," he said, spilling his runny cursive across the napkin.

Paul scrolled through his radio tuner's presets. "Solid."

Ted inked a *4* and then wrapped it in a tight circle. "My shitty-ass job. *SportsCenter.*"

"*SportsCenter?*"

"Yup," Ted said confidently. "The eleven o'clock. And pizza is six."

"You're struggling."

"My Higher Power counts?" Ted asked.

"Heck, yeah."

"Girls."

"All of them?" Paul said.

"Yeah, I guess so."

"Fair enough."

Ted flipped the napkin and scratched a *9*. "Ball—"

"I gave you *SportsCenter*," Paul began.

"Watching basketball," Ted continued without lifting his gaze from the napkin.

Paul raised his index finger. "Nearly there."

Ted nodded and spelled the letters *TEN*. "You."

"I'm not helping you make the list."

"No, I meant *you*," Ted said, grinning and folding the napkin into his pocket.

"You're a natural freaking charmer, Ted. Anyone ever tell you that?" Paul laughed and twisted the radio's volume knob.

"No." He opened the passenger-side door and stepped onto the asphalt. "Thanks for the ride."

Ted searched his pockets for his house key and swung open the screen door. Checking his Casio, he remembered that his mother's shift ended at ten. His mother was the head cashier at the Home Depot on 103, and his father had been the security supervisor there for the last five years. Their house was filled with complimentary mugs, magnets, towels, and pens, and Ted barely noticed the orange logo anymore.

Walking across the kitchen tiles, he paused in front of the refrigerator. Stuck to the freezer door was a pink Post-it note with his father's handwriting. Ted's old teammate Drew had called to leave his new dorm number. He squeezed the sheet of paper into a spitball and banked it into the garbage can.

Angrily swinging open the refrigerator door, Ted scanned the top shelf. He debated a Saran-wrapped plate of chicken salad and then spotted a chocolate cupcake sitting directly behind it. The cupcake was dressed with a thick coat of white frosting and a magenta birthday candle. He smiled at his mother's persistence. All week she'd been nagging him about a ninety-day-anniversary cake.

Ted walked out of the kitchen and down the hallway to his parents' bedroom. Knocking gently on the wooden door, he gazed across the cool ink shadows to his father's sleepy frame.

"I'm back," Ted whispered, double-checking his Casio. His father's Thursday late shift started at midnight. "I'm going to watch the Lakers game."

His father blinked at the slit of hallway light. "I'm getting up at eleven."

"Okay," Ted said, and swept the door closed.

As Ted crossed back through the foyer, he heard the door knocker clang against the strike plate. All of his parents' friends used the doorbell, and he wondered if he'd misheard the noise.

Ted jerked open the front door and stared through the screen at a wiry, olive-skinned man with a jagged widow's peak. He was wearing a navy blazer and a starched white oxford, and he had his hands casually balanced in the pockets of his khaki pants. He smiled warmly at Ted, like they'd known each other for years.

"You are beautiful," the man said, hanging on to the last syllable. He had a strong accent that Ted guessed was British or Australian. "Michael Esmer."

"Excuse me?" Ted began. Over Michael's shoulder, Ted could see a gray Jaguar parked against the curb.

Michael slid out his left hand and framed Ted's head shot with his thumb and forefinger. "That black-and-white you sent in doesn't do you justice."

"My dad's asleep, so—"

"I work with your university," Michael interrupted, "and I absolutely need to talk with you about your bright, bright future."

Ted studied Michael's enthusiastic grin. He'd figured on a wealthy Jesus freak or maybe a realtor. "What's there to talk about?"

"I have an offer, my Aquarian friend, that I think you will be very interested in."

Ted scratched his stomach, trying to remember the name of the admissions officer who'd called to say his first-semester payment was two weeks overdue.

"You're not a talker," Michael continued, gripping the screen door. Before Ted could invite him inside, Michael was standing on the wall-to-wall carpeting. Ted felt a rush of anxiety and then quickly decided he could take him, even with one knee. "But that's fine, fine with me, Ted, because I'm a talker by nature."

"I guess I don't understand," Ted said, annoyed.

"If you have a Diet Coke and ten minutes, I'll tell you all about it." Michael pressed his soft palm against Ted's elbow. "Which way to the kitchen?"

"That way," he said, gesturing over his shoulder.

Ted followed Michael's stride onto the kitchen tiles, studying his relaxed step. Ted's gift as an outside shooter began with his ability to read people's bodies. By junior high, he'd realized he could read the slope of a guard's shoulders, the curvature of a center's back, the tipped angle of a forward's chin, and intuitively know his next move. Bodies never lied, and most of the time Ted felt like he learned more from a person's balance than from his words.

Michael swung open the refrigerator door and searched the shelves with a concerned grimace.

"I think we have Diet Pepsi," Ted said, walking over to the pantry closet and twisting a can off a six-pack. "But it's warm."

"Actually I prefer Diet Pepsi warm." Michael dragged a chair away from the kitchen table and sat down with his chest facing the backrest. "It's an odd thing, but I'm not the only boy who does."

"My mother's the same way," Ted said, surprised. "How come Coach Pritchard never mentioned your name or anything?"

"Oh, is he the basketball guy?" Michael lifted the can and swallowed generously. "Well, luckily for you, Ted, that coach is the least important person in your universe. No, we're on to much bigger, better things."

Ted nodded and crossed his arms expectantly. He knew that sometimes the best response was no response at all.

"What would you say if I offered you another free ride through college?"

"In case you haven't heard," Ted said sarcastically, "my right knee is made out of metal."

"Yes, my friend, but your heart is gold, and that's the business—"

"But I can't jump," Ted shouted. Some days he wished he'd just lost the leg. Then none of the coaches would call; none of his friends would wish him luck.

"Ted," Michael insisted, raising his palm. "My offer has nothing to do with sport."

"Then—"

"I run a very small company, which works for a very rich man, and this very rich man is prepared to offer you a very free ride."

Ted pushed himself up onto the kitchen countertop. "And who would do that?"

"The 'who' is an excellent, excellent question, but unfortunately, and for reasons that will soon be all too obvious, it's a question that must remain unanswered." Michael reached into his breast pocket and removed a sheet of mint Nicorette gum. Splitting off a perforated square, he popped the yellow pellet into his mouth. "My purpose is to explain the whats and whys and then see if you're still interested."

"But that doesn't make any sense," Ted confessed.

"Well," Michael asked, "are you interested in going to college for free?"

"Yes, but—"

"No buts," Michael said, waving the Diet Pepsi can. "All I need to hear is that simplest of words, *yes*."

"Where are you from?"

"Originally, Cyprus. Moved to Wales at four, Germany for my concupiscence, and then I took my degree at University College, London. But I'm digressing," Michael said, vigorously chewing the Nicorette. "I'm here to say that you are the finest candidate we have for a specific, one-time-only scholarship."

"Then I'm interested, I think."

"In order to be eligible for, shall we say, final-round interviews,

I need to know if you'd be willing to participate in all aspects of this scholarship."

"Fine print," Ted muttered.

Michael smiled and flicked the tab on his soda can. "No, well, actually we're still very much in the large print, my Lothario. Our recipient will need to perform one clearly defined service."

Ted gripped the Formica countertop. Whatever it was they needed done, he was pretty sure somebody else could do it better.

Michael rested his forearms on top of the chair's backrest. "All you have to do is look out for a certain girl."

"What—?"

"Think of yourself as a big brother, a guardian angel, a best pal. Someone who can let us know how she's settling in, et cetera, et cetera."

"What are you talking about?"

"Just for your freshman year," Michael continued. "The next three years are yours to do with as you please. All tuition paid, no obligations whatsoever."

"You don't work for the college," Ted declared.

"Technically, no. Again, I run a small company in Manhattan, about which I'm happy to tell you anything and everything. But first I need to make sure you're the right guy for us."

"But I still don't understand."

Michael smiled sympathetically. "My guess is that you understand perfectly well. It's simply a question of coming to believe, and let me assure you, Ted, I'm quite real."

"You're telling me that a girl's willing to pay a hundred and thirty thousand dollars for a friend?"

"Yes and no. From your perspective, yes. From hers, no."

"You mean she wouldn't even know?" Ted asked incredulously.

"No," Michael said flatly. "You'd be working for her father, a university alumnus for whom tuition is simply not an issue. You may remember me mentioning a very rich man."

"This is a con," Ted said. "I—"

"Quite the opposite," Michael announced. "Actually, given your current predicament, I'd say this is the second chance of a lifetime."

"But this doesn't happen."

"Doesn't happen?" Michael repeated.

"I mean people don't . . ."

Michael shrugged. "Don't what?"

"And why would she even need—"

"She's a troubled, troubled girl, Ted. Medically speaking, she suffers from quite a severe case of bulimia nervosa, or simply, bulimia." Michael rattled his leather soles against the floor. "And her father is exceedingly worried about her being on her own for the first time. So worried," he drawled, "he's willing to lift you from the proverbial trash heap you've just landed yourself in."

"So what if she hates me?" Ted asked.

"Let's be realistic. This isn't mission impossible for someone of your . . ."

"What?"

"Attributes," Michael said, grinning.

"I think I'll probably reapply next year and go to State."

"So you'd rather pay fifty thousand dollars, get a degree they practically Xerox, and end up working next to your parents at the Home Depot." Michael placed the empty Diet Pepsi can on the kitchen table. "And to answer the question that's racing around your brain, yes, I've done my homework."

"What would I even say to my folks?" Ted asked, suddenly exhausted.

"Tell them it's a new alumni association scholarship or work-study, something vague. I have a drawer full of university stationery, and we can easily craft an official-sounding letter."

"I couldn't do that to them," Ted whispered.

"You feel you owe them more?"

Ted nodded.

"I understand." Michael smoothed his widow's peak with his palm. "If it helps, you should know that you and I share a common story, something quite elemental, actually."

"Yeah?"

"Well, neither of us knew our parents."

"I know my parents pretty well," Ted said.

"Yes, of course you do, but what I meant is that both of us were adopted. In your case, at a much earlier age than my own, practically a newborn, whereas I was left to my cousins—"

"How the fuck do you know all this?" Ted said, standing up.

"Your college recommendations," Michael explained, splaying his hands defensively. "Your English teacher, a Mrs. Rawls, wrote rather glowingly of your personal essays. Specifically, your essay on the decision not to seek the name of your biological mother."

Ted shook his head. He didn't like to think of himself as adopted, even though technically, Ted knew that he was. He'd spent as much time with his family as every other kid he knew, give or take a day or two. "And what the fuck does that have to do with anything?"

"Well, we're sons of chance, my friend."

"I'm the son of Jeff and Elaine," Ted said confidently.

"Fortune guided us on extraordinary paths in extraordinary ways. My proposal is no more random—"

"But why me?"

Michael crossed his legs tightly and brushed his kneecap. "In a world where everything can and will happen," he began, "the better question is 'Why not me?'"

Date: Thursday, 14 Aug 22:31:33
From: MichaelFIN@Highsmith.com
To: CharlesFIN@Highsmith.com

Many Cheers,

I am neither a fisherman nor a Hemingway enthusiast, but the tableau that best captures my evening's meeting with Ted York is that of the paroxysmal swordfish, splashing above the sea swells, setting the barbed hook. Where my previous interviews had faltered at the very sounds of their shrill voices, tonight, I knew almost instantaneously that our search was at a triumphant end.

Ted, a celebrated McDonald's All-American basketball player, was set to be the recipient of a series of grants from The John Little Foundation for Academic Enrichment. As you may know, Ivy League schools are forbidden from offering purely 'athletic' scholarships, and often circumvent this prohibition with private, under-the-table generosities. Unfortunately, or perhaps we might say fortunately, Ted's boosters abruptly deserted him after a near-fatal car crash left him with a prosthetic knee. To date, the University Financial Aid Office has been entirely unsympathetic to Ted's last-minute petitioning.

Shy and disarmingly handsome, betrayed and understandably shaken, Ted was immediately suspicious of our proposal. After his initial mistrust waned, however, I explained that while he possessed a bouquet of characteristics that would otherwise recommend him to us, he is in fact one of only a handful of matriculated students without any financial preparations to actually enroll.

To his credit, and in a gesture of obvious interest, Ted proceeded to deftly cross-examine our scholarship and its natural ambiguities. Regrettably, and due almost entirely to my wandering eyes, I was forced to reassure him at several points that his position would be absolutely and completely platonic. Though if cosmic forces are ever kind enough to assign me a guardian angel, I do ask that he also be a 6'3" brunette with saucer pecs.

Leaving Ted's house, I was exceedingly confident we'd seduced him with the idea of a second private scholarship. In many ways, in fact, the boosters' grants provided the perfect psychological primer for an offer such as ours. Ted and I are scheduled to talk tomorrow, and I presume he'll continue to pester me on the logistics and terms of our proposal.

Fortune is smiling gladly on us. You may expect an email from me by tomorrow afternoon.

Fingers Crossed,
Michael

Erica reached underneath her box spring and felt for the lip of her Ziploc bag. Since June, she'd been storing her CHEERIOS T-shirt behind a layer of plastic. The faded yellow cotton was speckled with fingerprint stains, and a bag managed to seal the sharp odor. She hand-washed the T-shirt in her sink every two weeks, but the fibers seemed to have absorbed the stench.

Erica stepped into her bathroom, twirled her hair into a pony-tail, and fastened it with a scrunchie. Sliding her Tank ring onto the marble vanity of the sink, she stared down at the thick band. She'd given up perfume a few weeks ago, and she couldn't decide if she could get away with wearing nice jewelry anymore. Jewelry was definitely next to go.

Instinctively surveying her forehead, Erica smiled at the top of the sink mirror. Last night she'd taken a bottle of nail polish and repainted a quote across the mirror in thick letters: WITHOUT MUSIC LIFE WOULD BE A MISTAKE—NIETZSCHE. The first two times she'd used lipstick, and someone had cleaned it off within the day. She didn't know whether it was the housekeeper or her father or The Ferret, but they'd finally conceded.

Erica's cell phone rattled against her desk, and she walked back into her bedroom. The display pulsed L HOME.

"Hey, babe. One sec." Erica pulled the CHEERIOS T-shirt over her head.

"How are you, little Ms. Sparrow?" Laura began. Until Erica was fifteen, she and Laura had spent their summers at Sparrow's Nest Camp in Connecticut.

"Good," Erica said as she crossed through the living room and into the front hall. "My dad's being a dick about school."

"What else is new?" Laura groaned.

"Whatever. I'm getting out of this house." Erica double-locked the front door. She knew her father and The Ferret wouldn't be home until after midnight, but she needed to feel the dead bolt click.

"So did you read my essay?" Laura asked tentatively. "I mean, what I sent you was a draft—"

"No, it was good," Erica interrupted. "I only had a bunch of word changes and comma jazz. I tracked changes in the Word file."

"Cool, cool. Thanks as always. It's so stupid that they make you apply to writing seminars."

Erica walked into the kitchen and placed the three packages of Powdered Donettes on the counter. "Yeah, it's pretty ridiculous."

"So, I met a boy last night." Laura laughed. "I mean, sort of."

"Really," Erica drawled through a smile. "Dish."

"Well, you know how my aunt does that fund-raiser every year? At the Regis."

"Okay," Erica said, flipping on the mini-television and turning to the Weather Channel. She hated the rough sounds of chewing, so she rarely ate in complete silence. Sometimes in restaurants she'd hum softly to herself while she was grinding away.

"Well, I had to run this basketball booth or whatever. One of those hit-the-shot-and-win-stuff games."

Erica sighed melodramatically. "What people will do for a stuffed animal."

"Exactly, so there's this guy—"

"No kidding."

"And he's been watching me for at least half an hour. You know, just walking around, making long turns, acting fabulous. I mean he was pretty cute, and especially for this fair."

"It's all relative," Erica agreed, arranging the six-packs of Donettes on opposite sides of a dinner plate, like silverware. She pinched the plastic seal on the first package. Leaning forward, she placed her nose over the opening and silently inhaled the sweet fog of confectioners' sugar and fried dough.

"Totally." Laura giggled. "So he comes up to the booth and

hands me the five bucks, and his first shot is a joke. Like I don't even play basketball, and I—"

"Nerves." Erica slid the six Donettes onto the center of the plate and organized them in a semicircle. A thin film of powder gathered on her fingertips, but she always refused to lick them. She knew digestion began in the mouth.

"Right, but the next shot was a perfect *swish*," Laura imitated.

Erica stared down at the snow-flaked rings, wondering whether she wanted to eat one or two at a time. She split open the other two packages and carefully removed the Donettes. She didn't want to shake them out because they looked so fragile. If one of the Donettes broke, she knew it would ruin her entire presentation.

"And so he picks up the last ball, and then he turns to me and says, 'If I hit this shot, can I get your number?'"

"That's a nice line. What'd you say?" Erica had done all the calculations in her head at the Food Emporium: 18 Donettes, 1,080 calories, 54 grams of fat, 138 grams of carbohydrates, 12 grams of protein.

"I didn't know what to say!" Laura exclaimed. "So, I'm like, 'Sure,' and I swear he didn't come close to the backboard. I mean, worse than the first one."

"Brutal." Erica stepped through the maid's room and into the bathroom. Bending down on one knee, she opened the sink cabinet and grabbed the bottle of Comet and the toilet bowl brush.

"And, of course, he just walks away like nothing's even happened."

Erica lifted the toilet seat and scattered Comet into the basin. The ashen disinfectant sprinkled out of the canister, turning violet blue on the wet porcelain. "What else could he do?"

"So, whatever, an hour goes by or something like that, and then he comes strolling back to the booth and just picks up a basketball. And he starts to shoot, and then he turns to me and says, get this, 'How about we pretend I hit that shot?'"

"I like this guy," Erica said, scrubbing the inside of the toilet bowl. It was essential that the porcelain surface be spotless. The only smell she would tolerate was the astringent punch of bleach.

"So I gave him my cell number," Laura finished. "But he hasn't called."

"He will."

"I mean, I figure—"

"He's got to wait a day or two, right?" Erica said, hesitating. She flushed the toilet and started back to the kitchen.

"What was that?"

"Oh, sorry," Erica said, startled. "I peed."

"No worries."

"So what else is going on?" Erica lifted the kitchen phone and punched in her own cell-phone number.

"Not much. Got that Tori bootleg that I—"

Call-waiting chopped the end of Laura's sentence.

"Oh, fuck," Erica said. "Can I call you back in a few?"

"No prob."

Dropping her cell phone onto the cutting board, Erica washed her hands and grabbed a glass from the drying rack. She filled the glass with tap water and placed it next to her dinner plate of Donettes. Then she did a mental spot check: shirt, front door, television, toilet bowl, water, and hands. She was ready, and, for the first time all day, she felt completely calm.

She keyed eight minutes into the microwave timer and watched the starting line flash. When the buzzer sounded, time was up. Pressing START, Erica reached for the first Donette. The sweet chalk absorbed all the saliva in her mouth. Her teeth mashed the dough into syrupy soil. She gripped the marble countertop and waited for the blood-sugar spike. It felt like an electric pulse, rising through the ceramic kitchen tiles, shooting up her calves and hamstrings, spiraling around her belly, and sizzling the back of her brain.

Erica stabbed her thumbs into the centers of a pair of Donettes and tucked one behind each cheek. She took a full swig from the water glass and lazily tilted her head back. Closing her eyes, she ran her tongue around her gums and gently dislodged scoops of Donette and caked sugar.

She worked counterclockwise around the circle, the evaporating trail of Donettes reminding her of a dynamite fuse from old Road Runner cartoons. Halfway through, Erica liked to stop and fight the creeping dizzies and the rising nausea. For some reason, they always seemed to want to wrestle. The dizzies were fun to brush off, but the nausea only got worse.

In the middle of the eighth Donette, Erica's molars sliced into her left cheek and glazed her tongue with blood. It was impossible for her to fully lose herself in the dough and sugar and still watch her chewing. She almost took it for granted that she'd bite her gums or lips eventually. Her tongue tickled the loose flame of skin and then welcomed numbers nine and ten.

By the time Erica picked up the eighteenth Donette, she felt like she was drunk. The weatherman seemed to be talking at half speed, the kitchen lights were dull and then blinding, the countertop was freezing her hands. She had to burp, but she liked bottling the pressure in her chest, just behind her breastbone. She'd waited all day to feel this disoriented and full and blank.

The double beep of the microwave startled Erica out of her daze. She looked down at the empty dinner plate and skimmed her fingers through the sugar dust. Sucking her fingertips, she started for the bathroom. Erica had tried everything from three to twenty minutes, and eight offered the perfect balance. She needed to be able to see the food exit but not before the sugar rush smacked her in the face.

Bending down on both knees, Erica leaned over the toilet bowl and breathed in fresh Comet. She wasn't sure she'd had enough water, but she was ready to try. Stretching her jaw into a silent scream, she reached into her mouth. Her finger flickered against her spongy tonsils and stroked the mucus at the back of her throat. The muscles in her face contracted, clutching her cheekbones. Pressurized waves rocked her sinuses, and she felt her skull cracking out of its skin shell. Erica's hands shook against the toilet bowl, and her throat whipped inside her rib cage. A splattering of Donettes leaped from her mouth and splashed into the shallow pool.

A second surge poured water and sugared fragments into the basin. As she tilted forward, stalactites of saliva stretched from her lower lip and landed on the mounting pile. Erica blinked away tears and waited for her chest to inflate. Her throat felt scraped and dry, and she tried to ignore the rotted scent that was flooding her nose and mouth.

A third swell shook her torso and sprayed muddy chunks of paste across the far wall of the bowl. Erica sat back on her knees and listened to her pulse thud. Her fingers and toes were twitching with energy, and she stared at the dime of blood that had settled atop the mass. She burped into her palm and sleepily stretched her neck in a full circle. Leaning back against the bathroom wall, she felt her entire body relax. Sinuses wide open and humming, chest swollen, eyelids halfway closed and purposeless.

Erica flushed the toilet and turned on the sink's cold-water tap. Running her pointer finger underneath the stream, she remembered the young doctor at East Hampton Memorial asking her what it felt like to binge and purge. She'd said she'd think about it and get back to him, but she'd known right away. Erica couldn't say it felt like having three orgasms in a row.

Date: Thursday, 14 Aug 23:04:52
From: CharlesFIN@Highsmith.com
To: MichaelFIN@Highsmith.com

M—Like the 10,000 ft overview. Would've preferred a girl but this kid sounds coachable. Will still need to do my own due diligence. Assuming all goes well, shoot him down here for a face-to-face. I think my words, my instructions, will clear the air. Cut the gay crap with this kid. Don't care where you put your pecker, but don't like that shit. Makes us/you seem less serious.—C

Ted's father dipped his razor in the sink's pool of milky water and then scraped away his charcoal sideburns. "Yorks don't lie to people. It's just not something we do."

"But he's not asking me to lie to anybody." Ted leaned against the bathroom door frame. "I mean—"

His father glared at him in the fogged reflection of the mirror. "Don't bullshit me, Ted."

"I'm just saying it's not like I have to be something I'm not." In the hour after his conversation with Michael, Ted had made a bargain with himself. If a man's character is the sum of his actions, then he could spend ten minutes a week working for Michael and still be a good person. As Paul said, "Recovery's progress, not perfection," and going to school was definitely progress.

"So it's okay to let people use you?" Ted's father said, and pursed his lips for the razor. His right hand was missing the tip of his ring finger, like the clipped end of a cigar.

"They were using me just as much for ball, though, right? I mean, this would take a tenth of the time of practice and games or whatever."

Pulling a hand towel off the chrome towel rod, Ted's father brushed the flecks of shaving cream from his neck. Wrinkles decorated his forehead, but when he smiled he looked twenty-five again. "I didn't raise a kid for sale."

"But it would be exactly the same thing for you and Mom," Ted said, irritated. "'Cause nobody even fucking knows they pulled my ride anyway."

"Watch the language." He tossed the hand towel into the hamper.

"Sorry," Ted began again. "All I'm saying is that for you guys, I mean, it would be just as if I hadn't crashed the truck."

Ted's father spun around on his heels and leaned back against the sink. Crossing his thick biceps across his chest, he shook his head. "You don't really believe that, do you?"

"No," Ted muttered.

"Good." His father waved him back into the bedroom. "Get me a butt out of my sock drawer."

Ted pulled open his father's dresser and dug through a mound of white athletic socks. Squeezing the Carlton soft pack, he tapped a cigarette into his palm and reburied the pack. "It's just that you didn't walk around that campus," Ted said, handing him the cigarette. "I mean, it looked like heaven, Dad. And what am I doing . . ."

Running his fingers along the top of the mirror, Ted's father dislodged a book of matches, lit the cigarette, and pulled a full drag. "Close the door," he said, switching on the exhaust fan.

Ted shut the bathroom door and sat down on the plush toilet-seat cover.

"Now . . ." His father exhaled. "Start from the beginning again."

"Okay," Ted said, grinning. "They're called FIN. Friends-in-Need Associates or Incorporated or something."

"And they've been doing this wacko stuff for years?"

"Yeah, I guess it's a New York thing."

"What a scam." Reaching behind his back, his father ashed the cigarette into the drain. "So then why come after you?"

Ted shrugged. "I guess 'cause they need somebody who's already enrolled or whatever. You know, someone who's in."

"But how'd they even hear about you?"

"Supposedly, this rich dad guy is some major donor. Some big-fish type that's given gazillions to the school."

Ted's father stabbed the cigarette against the marble and handed it back to his son. Ted sat up, dropped the smoldering butt into the toilet, and cranked the flush lever.

"There's no such thing as a free lunch." His father fastened the leather band of his Swiss Army watch. "And I'm late for work."

"But I'd be looking out for this girl—"

"Ted," he interrupted. "There are no free lunches. Nothing's that simple."

Ted swung open the bathroom door and collapsed on his parents' bed. "You don't care."

"I don't care?" he repeated, and yanked his Home Depot dress shirt off the dry-cleaning hanger. "Ted," he continued, staring down at his son. "Nobody wants more for you than me. Nobody."

"I know," Ted whispered.

"After those creeps pulled your scholarship, I was the one who had the ReMax agent come over here and take a look at this place."

"I'm sorry. I've just never wanted—"

"But with everything that's going on in your life, with drinking," Ted's father said, snapping together the buttons on his shirt, "maybe sticking around home is the safest thing for now—"

"Dad," Ted pleaded, and sat up. "I swear, if you let me go I'll stay clean. I'll go to meetings. I'll—"

"You can't make that promise," he declared. "Your mother's done a lot of reading about alcoholism and . . ."

Ted clapped his hands together prayerfully. "I'm making you that promise, Dad."

His father shook his head in disbelief and readjusted his watchband. "When are you supposed to talk to him again?"

Date: Thursday, 14 Aug 23:22:08
From: MichaelFIN@Highsmith.com
To: CharlesFIN@Highsmith.com

Cheers,

Before discussing the day's affairs, I must address the intolerant flare in your recent communiqué. Unlike the vast majority of my corporate contemporaries, I refuse to mistake sternness for seriousness. As you know, I have established a lucrative trade in the human arts, and it is my sincere belief that my associates and customers, yourself included, are suitably impressed with my committed service. With six flawless assignments between us, I should think you might resist the temptation to question my unconventional methodology. There are no limits to my professional devotion, ethical or legal.

Finally, if you are compelled to label my sexual orientation, I would appreciate the moniker 'bisexual.' Unlike you, and your predilection for busty blondes, I am captivated by the human spirit, rather than its ephemeral form.

More importantly, I just got off a call with a very eager Ted York. Ted will arrive at your office at 1:00 pm on Saturday. I will provide him with $1,500 for plane and cab fare, modest hotel accommodations, restaurants and entertainment, and wardrobe. In my expense memo, you may find the sum located under 'Retainer.'

Seriously Yours,
Michael

Date: Thursday, 14 Aug 23:40:44
From: CharlesFIN@Highsmith.com
To: MichaelFIN@Highsmith.com

M—Don't type this a lot: I STAND CORRECTED. Previous jobs were flawless. If the kid's everything you say, I have no right to question your methods. Once we're locked and loaded on the boy, you'll get the green. Shouldn't take more than 48 hrs to land on your beach.

One question: If I pass on Tiny Tim, he'll still know my name, my daughter's, yours. How do we guarantee his silence going forward?—C

Rocking her forearm steadily back and forth, Erica stared at the blackened images seesawing through the LCD display of her

Canon digital camera. The blood and lime power meters on her laptop and cell charger lit the carpeting like a miniature landing strip. She braced the viewfinder against her cheekbone and focused on the gumball screen saver ricocheting around her seventeen-inch laptop. Twisting the telephoto lens, she zoomed in and cropped the image with the plastic border of the screen.

The flash hissed, and Erica watched the hot light burn aqua haloes around her desk. She dropped the camera to her waist and studied the charcoal picture on the LCD. The flash had scorched an oval through the center of the display, speckling outward in a dust storm, and she instantly decided to spend the rest of the evening crafting her own personal galaxies.

The front-door hinges whined. Footsteps clattered on the living room's parquetry.

Erica quickly switched off the bedside light. Laying the camera on her nightstand, she reached over and set the clock-radio alarm for 9:15 A.M. She flipped her striped pillowcases and leaned back into the frosty cotton. Pico, The Ferret's bronzed Abyssinian, lazily pawed at the window ledge, and Erica watched the soft light of the screen saver infusing his cobalt eyes.

The cat hopped down to the carpeting and scratched his nails through the weave near the door frame. Erica rolled across her bed and met Pico's expectant stare. If she let the cat out, she knew her father would hear her door. If not, The Ferret would half-knock and then just walk right in.

She grabbed a handful of her comforter and rewrapped her torso. Waiting for The Ferret's stiletto drumroll, Erica gazed down at the stubby black hairs pushing through her calves. She debated resetting her alarm for 9:05 A.M., adding the necessary ten minutes to her shower, but she knew she'd just keep hitting SNOOZE.

The dull thud of fingertips scaled across the center of Erica's door, and she wearily shook her head.

"Yeah," Erica groaned.

The glass doorknob swiveled, and the hallway fixtures backlit Charles's ruddy smile. "Hey, team." He clamped his pudgy fingers around the thick of the door and winked at Pico.

"You look pleased with yourself," Erica said as she watched Pico dart out between Charles's pinstriped legs.

He shrugged nonchalantly and popped the collar stays from his starched dress shirt. "Picked it up at a fire-sale price," he declared, massaging his swollen belly. Since Erica was twelve, she'd referred to Charles's spherical gut as her Brother-to-Be. "Two hundred on the nose."

Erica drew the comforter to her chin. "I'm happy for you."

"You want to see the catalog—"

"I'm tired."

"In the morning," Charles agreed, nodding.

"Okay," Erica finished.

"And we can wrap up the college business—"

"What's there left to talk about?"

"I just want you to know," Charles began, "that I put a down payment on that NYU spot we talked about."

"What are you talking about?"

"Worst case: I eat a thousand-dollar loss." Reaching over to Erica's bookshelf, Charles ran his finger down the disjointed stack of CD jewel cases. "So I figure it's worth it to keep all of your options wide open."

Erica jerked upright, clutching the hem of the comforter to her breast, and flipped the bedside lamp back on. "Dad," she began incredulously, "you can't matriculate at two schools. They're both going to rescind my—"

"No, no, no," Charles interrupted. "Steven Douglas is best friends with the head of NYU's alumni association, and I gave him the fifty-thousand-foot overview. They're on board. Happy to help as option number two."

Erica fell back against the bed and draped her right arm across her face, blanketing her eyes.

"Kiddo, options are a good thing."

She pressed her forearm against her eyelids and watched paisley fractals stream through her field of vision. "I just want to go to sleep."

"I don't expect thank-yous, Erica, but I'm on your side here. How bad a school can it be if Laura's—"

"I didn't ask you to do this," she explained in a deliberate monotone. "I'm not happy that you did."

"Erica, every father wants their kid to go to their alma mater, but I refuse to let you . . ." Charles's voice faded as he rested his wrinkled brow against the door frame.

"What?" Erica whispered into the soft fold of her inner elbow. "What are you so afraid of?"

"Erica," Charles pleaded. "It's—"

"To see me dance?" she sang mockingly. "See me read? See me drink a beer?"

Charles grabbed the pile of CDs off the shelf and stared down at the spines. As he flipped angrily through the stack, PJ Harvey's *Dry* slipped through his fingers and clattered against the floor.

"To see me laugh," Erica continued. "Or see me—"

"Fail!" Charles cried. He bent down to retrieve the jewel case. "I don't want to see you fail at anything or—"

A deflated laugh broke Erica's smile, and she dropped her arms to her sides. "Dad, this isn't some kind of test I can fail. This is my fucking life."

"I understand." Charles sighed. "But *you* have to understand that I work with a lot of the top guys at the school. I mean, Christ, my fund's managing sixty-five million dollars of the endowment."

"Dad, I have nothing to do with that."

"And what about July Fourth weekend?" Charles asked sternly. "Am I supposed to just sit back and hope—"

Erica shook her head dismissively. "That's not going to happen again."

Date: Friday, 15 Aug 07:11:42
From: MichaelFIN@Highsmith.com
To: CharlesFIN@Highsmith.com

Cheers,

While I am entirely confident in Ted's candidacy, I can also assure you that he bears none of the feathers of a canary. Always remember that my livelihood and your personal security are absolutely entwined. However, should our friend press his lips to a whistle, the metal in his knee will hardly compare with the anchor tied to his ankle.

Ciao,
Michael

Date: Friday, 15 Aug 09:43:06
From: CharlesFIN@Highsmith.com
To: MichaelFIN@Highsmith.com

M—Final comment not a viable option for me—C

Charles stepped off the elevator on the twenty-ninth floor of the Horizon building, a folded *New York Post* tucked underneath the armpit of his blazer. Ted followed a step behind in a pair of stiff gray slacks and the indigo sweater he'd purchased that morning at Old Navy. The first thing Ted smelled was Chinese food.

"How's that knee doing?" Charles asked.

"Hurt a bit on the plane, I guess," Ted said, studying the geometric pattern in the hallway carpeting. "But it's good."

"Well, I appreciate you shooting down here for this sit-down."

Ted nodded and slid his hands into his pants pockets. Michael's instructions were clear. "Not unless spoken to."

At the end of the hall, Charles pressed his back against frosted glass doors and flashed his magnetic bracelet over an ID scan. The doors buckled and opened onto a pile of takeout cartons. The building maintenance crew worked Monday–Friday, and over the weekend the analysts built a towering landfill of pizza boxes, Mexican fast food, and Chinese takeout.

Charles squatted down in front of the pile and inspected the lower tier of plastic containers. "Obviously, we need to make sure we're on the same page."

"Yes," Ted said, breathing through his mouth.

Charles lifted a brown paper bag with a syrupy glaze dripping from the bottom corner and tossed it onto the top of the heap. Leaning forward, he removed a half-eaten container of sesame chicken and slid it into the newspaper's protective crease. He wiped his palm against the plush carpet and then pushed himself back up.

"Of course," Charles said, clumsily regaining his balance, "you realize the sensitivities."

"Yes, sir."

Charles opened the door to the analyst bullpen and motioned for Ted to follow him inside. Ten cubicles were scattered across the windowless room, and four industrial-sized printers sat in the corners, softly purring. Charles led the way across the bullpen, his short legs tripping the trail of light sensors, and Ted listened to the *tick-tick* flicker of the panel lighting. At the far end of the room, Ted spotted a young man asleep in his cubicle. He was seated facing his desk, his keyboard resting on top of his monitor and his face pressed against a stack of annual reports.

Charles walked over to the young man's cubicle and knocked on the plastic wall. "Wei," he said, adjusting his grip on the *Post*. "You're a fucking star. You hear me, a fucking star."

Wei sat up, startled, and reached for a highlighter. "Good morning, Prakes."

As the managing partner of Peninsula Markets, Charles asked all the analysts to use his old Andover nickname. He felt it added camaraderie.

"You scrub that M&A model last night?" Charles asked.

Wei looked curiously over at Ted and wiped his nose. "Most of it. Still needs tweaks."

"You're a fucking stud," Charles said, pointing his finger directly at Wei's chest. "Plug-and-chug." He turned around and motioned Ted toward the bullpen exit.

Charles unlocked the door to his corner office and dropped the sesame chicken and the *Post* in the center of his bare desk. Every day before he left, Charles filed all of his loose papers and presentations and sprayed the oak surface with 3M desk cleaner. He loved watching the foam circles dilate into disinfected spheres.

"So," Charles began, walking over to his floor-to-ceiling windows. "You must be pretty pumped to have school back on again. When Michael told me your story, I knew you were our guy. It was just the right thing."

Ted stood in the doorway, wondering how anyone could possibly concentrate with that kind of a view. He'd imagined Mr. Prakers in a sparsely decorated office overlooking a large department store or mall, but the view was New York City.

"Thank you," Ted said, guessing at the correct response.

"Well, I'm thrilled we could right the wrong. Oh—" Charles paused, turning around. "Sorry. Come in and close the door." He tossed his blazer onto a black leather couch and swiveled his desk chair. "Grab a seat," he said, sitting down and gesturing to the two armchairs facing his desk.

"Thank you," Ted repeated.

"So what do you think of Michael?" Charles asked, smirking.

"He's very energetic." Michael had prepped Ted on every subject but himself.

"Amazing story, that guy," Charles declared. "You know both his parents were killed when he was three? Car bomb in Istanbul."

Ted shook his head. "I—"

"BOOM," Charles exhaled. "Raised by some Brit classics scholar. Second cousin or something." He slid open the top drawer of his desk and removed an ivory plastic box with a nylon hoop attached by a cord. Quickly folding his shirtsleeve above his left elbow, Charles slipped his stumpy forearm into the blood pressure monitor.

"He said he grew up all over," Ted offered, watching the neon display cycle through numeric combinations.

"He tell you he was a fucking spy?"

"No, he—"

"Yeah. You wouldn't believe it, but he spent ten years doing intelligence work for MI5."

The monitor whistled a sharp ring tone, and Charles scribbled a short note and dropped it into his shirt pocket. "Then he hops the pond and builds the perfect little cash cow. I mean, no overhead, no fixed expenses. Do you know how much it costs just to keep the lights on in this building?"

Ted followed Charles's eyes to the ceiling and then shrugged. "He says you're one of his best customers."

"Oh, I've been using FIN for years. Mostly filling tables at these fucking galas." Charles placed the monitor back into the desk drawer and popped the lid on the sesame chicken. Brushing away a wrinkled green pepper, he lifted a small slice of pale meat and slipped it inside his mouth. "Our clients are the whores of the charity circuit. They'd panic if they saw an empty seat. And Michael's pretty discreet about the private entertainment stuff."

"Sure."

Charles leaned over the takeout container and pinched another piece of chicken. "Michael told me you really gave him the third degree. Says you'd make a top-shelf attorney."

"I guess I didn't believe him at first," Ted began slowly. "I mean, I'd never heard of a job like this before—"

"Sure, sure," Charles agreed merrily. "But I'll tell you, when you've got eleven billion dollars in assets to look after, you need all the help you can get."

Ted nodded.

"I mean," Charles continued, grinning, "between our place here and in Vail and out on the Island, I've got nine people working for me full-time."

"That's a lot of people."

"Cooks, housekeepers, drivers, gardeners," Charles listed, licking the gelatinous sauce from his fingers. "And you'd still be amazed how much shit goes wrong." He reached underneath his desk and pulled out a two-liter bottle of raspberry Diet Rite. Unscrewing the cap, he tilted the bottle to his lips and swished the soda around like mouthwash.

Ted crossed his legs and tugged nervously at the crease in his slacks. "I guess stuff still breaks."

"You're telling me." Charles ran his tongue over his gums and swallowed. "Why don't I give you the download on Erica. I assume you've heard some of this."

"I know a little bit," Ted said softly. "From Michael."

"So you know she's bulimic or a binger or whatever the fuck they're calling it this week?"

"Yes, sir."

"Well, the sixty-second takeaway is that our maid's kid tipped us off about nine months ago. Rosario's son comes with her on Saturdays, and I guess the little guy started picking up the noises coming from Erica's room." Charles untwisted a paper clip and speared a piece of chicken like an hors d'oeuvre. "Long story short, Rosario comes to me crying, I confront Erica, and a week later her doctor and I get her a top-shelf headshrink."

Ted's hands clamped the grooved contours of his armrests. "Okay."

"And I'm thinking we're tackling the problem. She seems good. I mean, I may not know all the right things to say, but I can put together a good team for her. And then fucking July Fourth."

"Sir?"

Charles stabbed another chicken strip. "Fucking July Fourth. Six weeks after graduation, and top of her class, she collapses at the Racquet Club in East Hampton."

"Why?"

"Hypokalemic alkalosis," Charles explained. "She'd puked out all of her electrolytes, Ted. And I don't need to tell you how important that shit is for your system."

"No, sir," Ted agreed.

"I spent forty-eight hours thinking she had leukemia or lupus or something. And then I find out she's done the whole fucking thing to herself. I mean, when that doctor came out and told me the score, I was blindsided."

"What happened?"

"She walks out of the hospital on Monday like it's nothing."

"Is she?" Ted stuttered. "Is she okay?"

"She seems pretty good. I mean, we switched her onto this new headshrinker, this specialist guy and . . ."

"I guess we do the best we can," Ted offered.

Charles sank down in his chair and covered his eyes, like he was shielding them from the sun. His Adam's apple was quivering against the clenched muscles in his neck, and Ted watched as his lips puckered into pale slices. "Ted, I'm someone who makes a living analyzing performance, and I'm not going to smooth this out. I've been a fucking lemon of a father. Sure, I've been shorthanded since Erica's mother passed on, but—"

"She died?"

"Cancer," he said, sitting forward and resting his elbows on the desk. "Fifteen years ago, May."

"I'm sorry."

"Which is why I'm so focused on making this a good move for her. I just need to know someone's looking out for her in the beginning, making sure she's settling in, taking care of herself." Charles scratched at the plastic label on the Diet Rite bottle. "I mean, you seem like the right guy, and those first few months are huge. Especially for her, for a girl like Erica."

"Yes, sir."

Dropping his hands to his lap, Charles forced a cough. His brown eyes were glassy, and the tip of his nose had a crimson blush. "Sorry," Charles whispered. "I guess you can see how difficult this is for me."

Ted nodded and uncrossed his legs. He didn't know whether he was expected to leave the room or offer a hug.

"I'm not used to feeling so powerless," Charles continued. "Which is why I need you to help me."

"I—"

"I guess we both need help, right?" Charles said, looking up at Ted.

The phone console squeaked through a double ring. Charles stretched his neck and studied the caller ID display. "Fuck you, Matt." He sat back in his chair and spun around toward the window. Lifting a pewter picture frame, he swiveled back to Ted. Charles rested the metal rectangle against his gut and ran his fingers around the edges. "This is Erica," he said, offering the picture to Ted.

Ted placed his hand underneath the frame; she looked straight at him. It was late afternoon at an outdoor party, and Erica was sitting on a white cast-iron bench, smiling stiffly into the camera. Ted's eyes traced her curly black hair, her crossed legs and tensely upturned left ankle, her baggy fleece pullover. He imagined the awkward moment before the shutter's click and her immediate disgust, and Ted realized she was probably afraid of the camera and the crowd behind her and the coming dusk.

Date: Saturday, 16 Aug 15:32:41
From: CharlesFIN@Highsmith.com
To: MichaelFIN@Highsmith.com

M—We're live, baby! You're the fucking man. Got 22-year-old Malaysian analysts on revocable work visas that talk more than Ted. He's a natural watcher. Best part is that the boosters already sold him on the school. Feel great about the deal. Most important thing: we both need each other's help. Want him on the same floor as my girl. Not next-door neighbors, but close enough. Treat him well. Buy him shit. Want him one hundred percent on our team.—C

Date: Saturday, 16 Aug 16:03:56
From: MichaelFIN@Highsmith.com
To: CharlesFIN@Highsmith.com

Cheers,

I am lying here on my couch, gazing fondly at a headshot of our boy. He telephoned me following your meeting and explained that he would consider the deal consummated when he received a First Semester Paid-In-Full receipt from the University Bursar. Let us discuss logistics at a more appropriate time. I now plan on getting royally pickled.

Congratulations,
Michael

"How are you feeling?" Doctor Rudas asked, flipping open a blue college-ruled notebook.

Erica picked at a thin tear in her armchair's stitching and watched Doctor Rudas cross his swollen ankles. She'd decided he was a midnight snacker, canned goods or salty carbohydrates. "I'm going."

"Erica, I owe you an apology."

"I'm going to school."

"Before we discuss that, can I apologize to you?"

"Sure, why not. It'll be refreshing." Erica scanned his bookcase. She'd memorized every title on the top three shelves, and he was missing the red-and-white spine of *The Essential Guide to Prescription Drugs.*

"Last session, I had trouble listening to you." He sighed and scrunched his eyebrows. "What you said about my son scared me, and I didn't react as your psychiatrist. I reacted as a scared father."

Erica gazed expectantly into Doctor Rudas's pistachio eyes. His thick jaw had exhausted his cheeks into jowls, and the wrinkles crisscrossing his neck suddenly reminded her of interstate highways. "Okay. . . ."

"Instead of hearing your deeper point, which is my job, I behaved impulsively, harshly." Doctor Rudas had a habit of stressing basic, monosyllabic verbs, and it made Erica feel like she was eight again. "I just want you to know that I recognize my shortcomings, and it's not going to happen again."

"Thanks for the sentiment," Erica said calmly, "but I think you're still missing the point. I was talking to you, the father."

Doctor Rudas tilted his head back and tugged the hem of his sport coat. "But that's not why you're here, Erica. You're here to see a doctor, a psychiatrist."

Erica's fingernail snagged on a loop of microfibers and snapped the armchair's stitching. Her hand jerked forward. "I was trying to make the point, since you admit to missing it, that they're one-and-the-fucking same, doctor and dad. You're not some glowing sphere that sits here twenty-four/seven, three-sixty-five just listening to people. Why should—"

"I hear what you're saying," he said, pausing on each word. "But focusing on me is not going to help you."

Erica took a deep breath and tried to slow her pulse. The caramelized smell of Mrs. Roberts's Chanel No. 5 was still drifting through Doctor Rudas's office. On Saturdays, Mrs. Roberts had the appointment before Erica's, and it took the first half of her session for the perfume to fade.

"I can't stand this," she declared.

"What?"

Erica shoved her hands into the pockets of her stiff jeans and spun the wheel on her iPod. "Why do I keep trying to explain myself?"

"It's a good process."

"I'm going to college."

"Fine; let's talk about that," he offered.

"And if you keep trying to stop me," Erica continued, "I swear I'll call the cops on your son."

Doctor Rudas closed his notebook and chewed his concerned smile. "Erica, let's not keep doing this."

"I hear what you're saying," Erica said, slowly enunciating each syllable. "But I need to make sure *you* hear what *I'm* saying. Coppers, five-o, pigs, po-pos, at your doorstep, searching your house."

"Do you even want me to help you?"

Erica raked the denim grain of her thighs. She hated the way her stomach felt when she was sitting in his armchair. "I want you to get out of my way."

"Erica, assuming you do go to school, your father is still going to insist that we talk. I mean, he's—"

"I know," Erica muttered. "I'm sure you're looking forward to it as much as I am."

Doctor Rudas grinned. "And I'm also going to ask that you continue taking your mood stabilizer."

"Why don't you guys just call it Prozac?"

"Prozac," Doctor Rudas recited. "Fluoxetine hydrochloride. The Zac. Brain candy."

"So write me a prescription," Erica said, studying the cliché pictures on his desk. Doctor Rudas had a wooden five-photo frame of vacation sunsets. "For a month's worth of my shit with a hundred refills, and then forget about me."

"So you do believe in my psycho-pharmaceutical treatment?"

"Whatever it takes to get the fuck out of here."

"Then you can trust me to a certain extent?"

Erica smirked. "I can bargain with you, but I think you've already realized that."

"I appreciate the distinction," he conceded.

"You're kind of . . ." Erica paused. "Well, kind of like a drug pusher."

Doctor Rudas shook his head in disbelief and reached for his Paxil coffee mug. Over the last month, Erica had watched him refill it with club soda and Caffeine Free Diet Coke, but he sipped like he was scalding his tongue. "So you're of the opinion that my thirty years of psychiatric experience is of no use to you?"

"I don't think we're talking zero." Erica shrugged. "But it's a single-digit experience."

"In the past, you've said you enjoy being able to say whatever you want."

"I said 'single digits.'"

Doctor Rudas sat forward and laughed, and Erica was pretty sure it was the most honest emotion she'd ever seen him express. "I appreciate the vote of confidence."

"No problemo," she said hesitantly.

"I'll whistle all the way home."

Erica felt her low blood sugar blurring her focus, and she checked her watch. "I don't like beating a dead horse, but you did get my threat, right? I mean, I don't want to leave here with you thinking I was joking."

"What is it you're afraid I'll do?"

"Call my father again."

"I don't tell him what we discuss, Erica, but I will have to share my general medical opinion with him."

Erica nodded. "You get my point."

"I hear your point," Doctor Rudas said. "And I think you'll be pleased to know that I hear your threat as well."

"Sorry for being so blunt."

"Are you this direct with everybody?"

"No. Is it a problem for you?"

"I think it's very healthy, actually."

"I'm getting better by the minute," Erica whispered.

"And you're sure leaving for school in two weeks will continue this positive trend?"

"Good segue." Erica smiled at Doctor Rudas. "You might have broken ten percent with that one alone." On her walk home, Erica decided, she'd buy herself a bag of Swedish Fish. Either Swedish Fish or sour gummy bears. She knew she needed something to make it to dinner with her father and The Ferret, and she felt like she'd earned it. "I just need to get out of my house."

"I see. Do you understand why I'm discouraging such a major shift?"

Erica pouted her lower lip and playfully crossed her eyes. "Could it have something to do with the five thousand dollars a month you make off me?"

Doctor Rudas swiveled around to his desk and reached for his day planner. "Do you really believe that, or are you just trying to be provocative? Because if it'll help, I'll show you my waiting list." He lifted the leather notebook and rattled the pages suggestively. "My schedule will be full, with or without you."

"Then enlighten me."

"Well, as you know, bulimia and anorexia are very often—"

"I'm not fucking anorexic," Erica interrupted.

"Eating disorders as a general category," Doctor Rudas corrected.

"So you can put away your label maker."

"Erica—"

"I mean, do I look fucking anorexic?" Erica asked rhetorically.

"I wasn't trying to label you," Doctor Rudas insisted.

"Fine."

"Can I start again?"

Erica openly rechecked her watch. "Take two."

"Well, as I was saying, eating disorders are frequently cyclical. A person can go several weeks or months without exhibiting outward symptoms." He balanced his hands in the air like a conductor. "For example, an alcoholic can be dry for months at a time, sometimes even years, but there is always the danger that he or she will return to their destructive drinking behaviors."

"Is this how you keep your schedule so full?"

"My point is that there are peaks and valleys, manageable periods and unmanageable periods. While you seem to be in reasonably good spirits today, you, yourself, have admitted to being cyclically—"

"You're worried I've got another Racquet Club in me?"

"Well, aren't you?"

"Doctor Rudas," Erica said coolly, "the scariest thing in my life right now is being trapped at home."

 SEPTEMBER

Date: Monday, 1 Sep 00:53:10
From: MichaelFIN@Highsmith.com
To: TedFIN@Highsmith.com

Cheers,

I hope this note finds you comfortably settled in your dorm room.
Having scrupulously reviewed the building's floor plans, I can assure
you that your second-floor unit is among the most spacious and well-lit
doubles in the dorm. Additionally, E's double is conveniently located on
the opposing hallway, a hop, skip, and a jump through your stairwell.

As I mentioned during our last call, I have compiled a series of
communication guidelines or, if you'll forgive my braggadocio,
commandments. And just as Moses smashed his stone tablets, I ask
that you immediately delete this electronic prescription.

1) Only access Highsmith when you are alone in your dorm room and
you have locked your door.

2) Only access Highsmith from your personal computer (e.g. no computer clusters, cell phones, friends' computers).

3) Never bookmark Highsmith in your web browser, set Highsmith as your Homepage, or click the *Save Username* and *Password* icon.

4) Never write down or digitally store your Highsmith username, password, or email address.

5) Never click *Reply* when responding to a Highsmith email. Always compose your note in a blank message box.

6) Never save a copy of a Highsmith email to your Sent Mail Folder.

7) Never print out a Highsmith email.

8) Never digitally store a Highsmith email.

9) Never include a real address or identifiable landmark (e.g. bar/restaurant, museum, school building) in your Highsmith email.

10) Never use a person's full name in your Highsmith email, especially your own.

Please forgive my brusque language, for there are but few points on which my resolve is so absolute. Assuming you gladly honor the above suggestions, and I'm quite sure you will, I anticipate our weekly emails to be naturally chatty and informal. Of all my qualities and skills, I am, more than anything, a born gossip.

I should also add that I am certainly not expecting your emails to be high literature. Notes, random thoughts, and observations are all perfectly acceptable. I need the big picture, my friend, not a novel.

Lastly, if you need anything, anything at all, don't hesitate to include it in your communiqués. I make things happen.

Fondly,
Michael

Ted stood in the center of room 219, staring at the turkey. The bird's stout profile and unflinching pebble eye had been watching him unpack all afternoon, and Ted silently debated rotating his roommate's Wild Turkey bottle so that it faced the wall. Then he decided against it.

Ted had learned his roommate's name, James Zachary, from the purple construction paper taped to their door, but they still hadn't met. When Ted had arrived three hours ago, he'd found James's clothes scattered haphazardly across the left bed and the left desk. Ted hadn't cared about the mess or the bed choice. Instead, he'd stood there hypnotized by the meticulously built minibar.

James had carefully arranged six bottles of liquor on the middle shelf of his bookcase, and he'd backlit the glass containers by taping a short string of Christmas lights to the wall. The tiny beams refracted against the Wild Turkey's maple syrup, casting crisp, rhombic shadows along the carpeting. To the left of the Kentucky straight bourbon rested a squat container of Tanqueray gin. The bulbs infused the emerald bottle with an aquamarine glow, reminding Ted of fireflies, and then sea glass, and then oblivion.

Ted braced his cell phone against his shoulder and listened to the choppy ring.

"Yel-lo," Paul shouted.

"Hey," Ted said, relieved to hear Paul's stupid greeting. "My roommate's built a fucking booze altar." He reached into his army duffel and unpacked two picture frames: his parents at the Websters' annual barbecue and his senior-year starting five.

"What?"

"Like a bunch of bottles, with lights and—"

"It's called a bar," Paul interrupted.

"I think this is more than a bar."

Paul burst out laughing and fell into a smoker's cough.

"Whatever," Ted said, resurveying James's bulletin board. His roommate had decorated a large corkboard with overlapping summer snapshots. Ted had already tried to identify James in the collage of friends and hugs, but he'd only narrowed it down to three preppie suspects. The longer he stared at the images, the more they reminded him of the carefree world inside a Polo advertisement.

"You see an altar," Paul declared. "He sees a bar."

"This isn't just a bar," Ted insisted, and picked up his airmail tube of posters. Sliding out a low-angle shot of Chris Webber halfway through a reverse slam, he worked his fingers over the cracked edges. He'd won the poster at the Agricultural Fair when he was fourteen, and he'd been religiously repairing it ever since.

"Dude." Paul chuckled. "I'm sitting at a hella old wooden desk right now. I see a desk, but a termite would see a freaking buffet."

"So what the fuck do I do?"

"Simple," Paul continued. "Go to a freaking meeting. Go to two."

"That's not going to move these bottles."

"You think your HP had those guys give you back your scholarship 'cause He wanted you to drink?"

Ted sighed. "Maybe you're right."

The door hinges squeaked, and the metal knob bounced off the rubber doorstop. "I'll call you back," Ted whispered.

"I'm here for you, kid."

Ted turned around and met the bloodshot eyes of James Zachary.

James tossed his head back and gave Ted a crooked grin. "James," he said, reaching out to shake.

James was shorter than Ted had expected, five-seven or five-eight at the most. He was wearing a purple fleece, baggy cargo pants, and a pair of moldy Adidas flip-flops.

Ted squeezed his soft palm. "Ted."

"Where you from?"

"Outside Chicago, a bit. How about—"

"The city," James declared.

"Like New York?"

"Eight million strong. Real chill posters," James said, sitting down on the edge of his bed. His steady smile reminded Ted of a game-show host. "I brought Bob."

James had tacked a gigantic black-and-white Bob Marley poster over his bed. The photo was an early head shot, and Marley was releasing an enormous plume of pot smoke through a wide smile. His face and dreadlocks were in sharp focus, but the drifting smoke was blurring portions of the image and seemed a half second away from filling their dorm room.

Ted leaned awkwardly against his bedpost. "Must've taken a few minutes to hang—"

"And I brought the classic Dave." Above his desk, James had hung a poster of Dave Matthews Band's *Crash*.

"I brought *Born in the U.S.A.*, but I wasn't sure—"

"Right on." James nodded and pushed aside a towering pile of sweaters. "So you want to check out my brother's house?"

"Your brother goes here?" Ted asked, surprised.

James leaned over and slid open his desk drawer. "He's a senior in Sigma Chi. It's definitely the house for us to join," he said, grabbing a tin of Skoal Straight. "Lip?"

"I think I'm good for now."

James wrapped his thumb and finger around the tobacco hockey puck and snapped his wrist. "Well, we're going to break in my three-twenty later tonight," he said, pointing his thumb down Brook Street. "Present from the 'rents. For getting into this fucking joint."

"Three-twenty?"

"It's only a V-six," James explained, "but it's got two hundred and fifteen horses." He mimed a relaxed grip on the steering wheel. "Eighteen valve and that wicked navigation shit. We're going to need it out here in the sticks."

"Nice," Ted agreed, nodding.

"You should come with," James began excitedly.

Ted shrugged as casually as he could, and James's smile faded slightly. Ted suddenly felt like grabbing him by the collar and shouting, "I could drink you under the fucking table."

"I gotta get some of this stuff packed away," Ted said.

"I hear that." James stood up and brushed his fleece. "Well, we'll catch up later." He reached to shake again.

"Cool," Ted said, gripping James's hand more tightly than he meant to. In the moment, drinking seemed less frightening than unpacking alone.

"Late." James swung the door closed behind him.

Ted collapsed on his quilt and stared out the window. The sunlight was falling straight down on the New England pines, and somewhere he could smell leaves burning.

Stepping into the hallway, Ted traced his fingers along the grooved wall. The three other doors on his hall were all closed, and he tried to commit each paper placard to memory. JENNA & SUSAN, JASON & DANIEL, DEBBIE & STACY. At the end of the row, he found the bright orange door marked BATHROOM. He twisted the handle and felt the dead bolt stick.

"One second," a girl's voice sang out.

Ted snapped his hand back from the handle like he'd just been hit with a static shock. He wanted to walk quickly back to his room, but he worried that JENNA or SUSAN would spot him limping away. Dropping his head, he rehearsed a casual introduction.

The bathroom door swung open, and Ted immediately recognized her ankle from the photograph. He'd broken his talus going up for an offensive rebound, and he remembered the way Erica's left ankle joint was smaller than a pinball.

"It's all you," Erica said, holding the door open.

Ted jerked his chin to full attention and looked straight at her forehead. He was suddenly terrified of her eyes.

"Thanks," Ted mumbled as he stepped past her.

"Yup."

Gently closing the door, Ted took a hurried breath. "What the fuck am I doing?" he whispered.

Ted lifted the toilet seat, unzipped his fly, and stretched his arms toward the ceiling. "What the fuck am I doing?"

After flushing the toilet, Ted walked over to the cloudy marble sink and ran the cold water. He tilted forward and balanced his face inches from his reflection.

"You can do this," he said, trying to talk himself down. He slipped back onto his heels and dipped his hands into the gathering pool. As he lifted his eyes to the mirror again, the words seemed to dribble out of his mouth: "You can't do this."

Ted shut off the faucet and shook his hands in the air. He opened the bathroom door, flipped the light switch, and walked back down the hallway. As soon as he'd locked the door to his room, he slid his cell phone out of his jeans and scrolled to Michael's number.

The line rang once. "My darling, darling, Theodore, this is most unexpected."

"I—I—" Ted stuttered.

"Speak, my son, speak."

"I'm starting to think I can't do this," Ted said, pacing a small circle. "I can't do this."

"Okay," Michael said soothingly.

"I can't do this," Ted repeated.

"Can't do what?"

"What?"

"You said, 'I can't do this,' and I'm infinitely curious as to what 'this' is."

"This whole thing." Ted paused his loop on the verge of dizziness.

"Okay, but what part, specifically, can't you do?"

Ted shook his head furiously. "Probably everything."

"That's absurd," Michael answered. "You can go to class; you can study."

"Yes, but—"

"You can go to parties, hang out with—"

"I—" Ted started.

"And you can certainly send me an itsy-bitsy, teeny-weeny e-mail once a week saying our common friend is looking well or unwell."

"But what if I—"

"This is terrifically uninteresting," Michael said flatly.

"You need to listen to me," Ted yelled. His chest was shaking, and he could feel his undershirt sticking to his armpits.

"And you," Michael shouted, "are making a complete ass of yourself."

"I'm sorry."

"Ted, my friend, you have no conception of what backing out would mean."

"What?"

"It's impossible."

"Why?"

"Send the e-mails," Michael said in a mechanical monotone.

"I—"

"Send the fucking e-mails, Ted."

"I'm sorry," Ted began again. *Beep.* "Hello? Hello? Fuck."

Date: Monday, 1 Sep 18:42:48

From: MichaelFIN@Highsmith.com

To: TedFIN@Highsmith.com

Cheers,

I am completely willing to forgive and forget today's hysterics, if, after our chat, you feel fully exorcised of your pre-match jitters. While I was unsurprised by your sudden attack of nerves—I rather expected a bout of stage fright—I feel compelled to remind you of two very critical points. Firstly, your compensation package is absurdly generous. At ten minutes per week, twenty at most, we are simply asking for a sum-total of ten or twelve hours of your time. A day's work for $130,000 seems quite fair, does it not? Secondly, in my line of work, people honor their commitments.

Patiently,

Michael

Date: Monday, 1 Sep 22:50:18

From: TedFIN@Highsmith.com

To: MichaelFIN@Highsmith.com

I'm not a quitter either just so you know. I guess it was hard to see her and have it all be real like that. I bumped into E. leaving the bathroom. We barely said five words to each other but I remember her tone being real polite. I've walked by her room a couple times and she's got stuff all over the place. Her roommate looks a lot more settled in because I think she's a gymnast and she's been here a few extra days. I'm not sure about that but I remember her name from a list of recruits. That's all I've got for now. Sorry again about calling the emergency number.

T.

Date: Tuesday, 2 Sep 00:22:09
From: MichaelFIN@Highsmith.com
To: TedFIN@Highsmith.com

Cheers,

Now really, Mr. Aquarius, that wasn't so, so awful.

Expectantly,
Michael

_____

***ep149846 has joined the table
***You are host of this YAHOO CHESS table. This gives you the power to invite people to (or boot people from) your table. You may also limit other players' access to your table by selecting its 'Table Type.'
***DrMTRudas has joined the table
ep149846: s'up doc
DrMTRudas: Hello, Erica. I've never played chess online before!

ep149846: there's no privacy in this fucking dorm so I ixnayed the phone idea . . . we can chat here

DrMTRudas: Wouldn't AOL IM be simpler?

ep149846: pater familias knows my aol screenname . . . besides you can cut and paste ims and you can't here

DrMTRudas: I see. I didn't realize that was a concern.

ep149846: i offered to let you bill me w/o wasting your/my time

DrMTRudas: That would be fraud.

ep149846: when did you suddenly start worrying about being a fraud

DrMTRudas: Clever.

ep149846: it's your move btw

Date: Friday, 5 Sep 11:19:53
From: TedFIN@Highsmith.com
To: MichaelFIN@Highsmith.com

I don't think there's much to tell really. E. seems busy all the time but I probably seem busy too. Every time I see her she looks like she's late for a lecture. We're shopping classes right now so it's possible she's going to like twice as many classes as normal. I'm signed up for a history class, two intro math classes, and basic accounting. I figured you might want to know what you are paying for. I'll write more during the week if I notice anything or whatever.

T.

P.S. Thanks for the welcome care package from Student Services. I don't have a cousin M. so I knew it was you. I've already eaten both bags of Doritos.

Date: Saturday, 6 Sep 01:23:09
From: MichaelFIN@Highsmith.com
To: TedFIN@Highsmith.com

Cheers,

Bravo, my kind emissary! Your words, while occasionally sparse, are
incredibly helpful. How are you finding your new accommodations?

Thankfully,
Michael

Date: Sunday, 7 Sep 12:08:47
From: TedFIN@Highsmith.com
To: MichaelFIN@Highsmith.com

The school is really nice. My dorm is only a block away from the
athletic facility and it's probably the fanciest gym I've ever seen.
As long as I keep my leg straight I can do a lot of the different
machines and stuff. I also found the student lounge where they
keep all the ping pong and billiards tables and video games. In the
back they have a projection screen tv and they basically only show
the games that are on. The libraries are also really nice. There are
like twenty of them around campus and they all look like museums.
They make you feel like you are some sort of old scholar. Anyway
I'm still finding my way around.
T.

Erica walked down the second-floor hallway in her white terry-cloth bathrobe, making fists with her toes in the carpeting. Since 3:00 A.M., she'd been trying to wash out her roommate's snoring with her iPod's bootleg of Tori Amos's "Precious Things." The first thirty seconds of the track were built on jagged breathing, and Erica had spent the rest of the song mouthing the lyrics at Maisy Landrigan's gang of stuffed animals. *With their nine-inch nails, and little fascist panties/Tucked inside the heart of every nice girl.* Erica had decided that she could handle Maisy's gymnastics posters and her Case Logic of Jackson Browne, but at some point, she was convinced she was going to disembowel one of her room-mate's purple teddy bears.

Squinting at the fluorescent ceiling panels, Erica re-counted the four quarters in the front pocket of her bathrobe. She'd fallen in love with Fresca at Sparrow's Nest, and she'd decided it was an omen that the second-floor soda machine's bottom tab read FRESCA, in black marker. Fresca had the perfect zero-calorie bite without any of the caffeine.

As Erica passed room 215, she noticed that the door to the sec-ond-floor lounge was propped open. She hesitated for a second, tightening her belt, and then guessed that somebody had forgot-ten to loosen the doorstop. Stepping tentatively past the lounge doorway, she scanned the Chinese-blue couches. Erica instantly recognized the guy from the bathroom. He was lying out-stretched on one of the couches, dangling a maroon flip-flop from his big toe and scratching absently at his bare chest. A *Course Announcement Bulletin* was balanced on the elastic waistband of his warm-up pants.

Erica skipped hurriedly past his eyeline and then paused outside the door to the bathroom. She couldn't decide if she was embar-rassed by her messy ponytail or her swollen pores, but she suddenly felt like turning into the bathroom and meticulously inspecting herself. Erica quickly debated taking a circuitous, first-floor route back to her room and then decided against it. She knew he lived on the same wing, and she figured he'd be expecting a return trip. A no-show would suggest a hookup. Besides, he might spot her coming back up their stairwell, and then she'd feel like a fool.

Erica hit the FRESCA tab and listened to the can smack against the metal drop slot. Kneeling down, she flexed the tab on the soda and took a full sip. The bitter mélange of grapefruit and aspartame coated her stomach and, in an instant, she resolved to walk confidently back down the hallway. Boys were now part of the equation, even shirtless boys, and she was the only person who had the right to judge herself.

Ten feet from the lounge, Erica realized she'd instinctively refastened her ponytail, and it infuriated her. Reaching again for the elastic, she yanked it from her hair; it ricocheted off her robe, skipping silently across the carpeting.

Erica stepped into the lounge and leaned against the metal door frame. She'd been gathering foot speed since she left the soda machine, and she felt her torso sway forward into the room.

Ted sat up, startled, and pressed the pages of the *Course Announcement* to his chest.

"I can't sleep," Erica began. She'd wanted to say something clever or dry and suddenly found herself settling for the truth.

Ted swung his legs to the floor, still clutching the booklet to his skin. "Same," he said, waiting for her to shout "Liar."

"My roommate snores."

"Mine's never around." Ted watched her sit down on the opposing couch. His eyes traced the pale reservoirs of her neck down to her thin shoulders.

"Are you a light sleeper?" Erica asked hesitantly.

"I guess I probably am." Since the accident, Ted's sleep had been terrorized by basketball dreams. Last night his right leg had jackknifed on a breakaway layup. Tonight he'd suddenly healed himself, and nobody believed him.

"I don't mind car horns or city noises," she mused, "but people noises get me." Erica felt her thighs spread together against the terry cloth, swelling like loaves. She'd stolen the robe from her father's health club, and the fit was comfortably amorphous without being baggy. She needed enough fabric to wrap a tight V-neck front, and the length had to hang just below her ankles.

Ted let the *Course Announcement* fall to his lap. "I think my problem is more staying asleep."

"Not me," she said, consciously focusing on Ted's sharp jaw. "Once I'm out, I'm out."

"Are you a big dreamer or whatever?"

"Sometimes, yeah," Erica said.

"Well, I think I'm on one of those nightmare streaks. You know, like all sorts of weird stuff."

"That sucks," Erica said, peering down at her Fresca. She wished she'd bought a Sprite or ginger ale. If he noticed the diet soda, she was convinced he would start thinking about weight and calories. Erica sat back against the couch, angry with herself for drinking another Fresca, for worrying about buying something else, for thinking too much.

"It's exhausting," Ted confessed. A tingling itch burrowed into his scalp, but he didn't want to lift his arm and flash his pit. "But I guess it's probably better than listening to snoring."

"You ever try and trick yourself out of them?"

"Like before I fall asleep?"

Erica's eyes wandered across Ted's chest. "No, I mean *in* the dream."

"I don't think it would work for me," he said. "I mean, half the time, I'm in the thing, thinking *I wish this was a dream. Why isn't this—*"

"That's different," Erica interrupted. "I mean, like lucid dreams," she said softly, wishing she hadn't cut him off. "I'm not very good at them, but I tried it a couple years ago."

"Lucid dreams?" Ted repeated. He was convinced she'd already labeled him a moron.

"You can teach yourself how to control your dreams using these crazy techniques."

"Like what?"

"I can't remember them all, but the one I tried was with a piece of paper. This book said to carry around a little note and to reread it three times on the hour. Supposedly, you'll start doing this in your dreams. But in the dreams, the text will shift each time you read it, like morph. Then, you're in the dream, and you know you're dreaming."

"Did it work?" Ted pictured himself collapsed on a basketball court, desperately searching his pockets for a note.

"I had a few dreams where I was looking for the piece of paper, but I never actually found it."

"I probably couldn't handle that," Ted said, smiling.

Erica felt his grin shiver through her skin. She couldn't remember the last time she'd made a guy smile naturally. "I always think about trying it again."

Ted sat forward and scratched his cheek. "Wait, so what'd you write? I mean, on the note."

"It was stupid," she said, embarrassed.

"Why? I mean, you don't have to— Sorry, I shouldn't have

asked that sort of thing," he said, shaking his head apologetically.

Erica watched Ted's hand flinch closed, and she remembered the way he'd hidden his face from her outside the bathroom. "Just breathe," Erica declared.

"What?"

"That's what I wrote."

"Just breathe," Ted repeated.

"But it didn't work, so whatever," she said, yawning.

"Well, but maybe it did, right? I mean, I guess it could've, but you might not remember."

"Theoretically," Erica conceded. She placed her palms on the cushions and started to stand up. "I should probably try again with the sleeping thing."

"Right," Ted said, reaching for the *Course Announcement*. "I guess I'm going to keep flipping through this."

"Hey." Erica rested her hand back on the door frame. "I never asked you your name."

"Ted."

"I'm Erica."

"Cool," he said, nodding. "It was nice to—I mean—"

"Nice to meet you, too," Erica finished. "'Night."

_____

DrMTRudas: On a more serious note, would you mind if I asked you one or two questions while we played?

ep149846: can i have my last move back

DrMTRudas: I don't want to barter with you, Erica.

ep149846: a move for a question . . . i shouldn't have moved my bishop

DrMTRudas: Fine.

***undo requested by ep149846

DrMTRudas: How are you doing with your diet, meals, bingeing?

ep149846: you have to click 'okay'

DrMTRudas: Sorry.

***undo granted by DrMTRudas

ep149846: how do i know my answer will stay between us

DrMTRudas: You know because we both value our family privacy.

ep149846: fair point . . .

***check

DrMTRudas: Nice move.

ep149846: honestly i think the change of scenery is really helpful . . . there's zero privacy in a dorm and that makes all the other stuff kind of impossible

DrMTRudas: That's wonderful news!!! Do you mean you haven't binged since you arrived?

ep149846: sorry doc . . . you only bought yourself one question

DrMTRudas: Well, I'm sincerely happy for you, Erica.

ep149846: told you i had to get out of dodge . . . nice game

***checkmate

Date: Wednesday, 10 Sep 13:52:08
From: TedFIN@Highsmith.com
To: MichaelFIN@Highsmith.com

I bumped into E. in the kitchen/lounge late Tuesday night and we had our first real chat. We talked for like five minutes about sleeping habits and stuff like that and then she went back to her room. I'm glad she knows my name now. No other news on E. really but I've started to notice that she definitely has her patterns. When she works in the S. library she always sits at the back right corner table next to the magazines. I also keep seeing her with cans of fresca. We have a vending machine on the floor and she must buy three or four cans a day. Half the times I pass her in the hallway she's got a new one.

T.

Date: Thursday, 11 Sep 01:23:09
From: MichaelFIN@Highsmith.com
To: TedFIN@Highsmith.com

Cheers,

I'm quite happy that you and E are already on pleasant terms. It is a testament to your kind and gentle nature. Additionally, C and I both appreciate your use of pertinent details.

Gratefully,
Michael

Date: Saturday, 13 Sep 17:19:53
From: TedFIN@Highsmith.com
To: MichaelFIN@Highsmith.com

Not much to write really. E. likes to read in the lounge and eat rice cakes. The funny thing about the rice cakes is that she always builds this tall stack of like ten of them but I've never seen a bag or box or container with her ever. My roommate said it looked like the leaning tower of pisa and it was one of the only times I've agreed with him. I think I keep expecting her to do or say something real crazy but she seems kind of focused. To be honest I don't really understand what I'm supposed to be doing for you. I mean I could write the same email about five other people on my floor or whatever.

T.

Date: Saturday, 13 Sep 21:23:09
From: MichaelFIN@Highsmith.com
To: TedFIN@Highsmith.com

Cheers,

Do not despair, young Theodore!!! Your vigilant reporting provides our patron with daily reassurances. As I've said before, our boss views us as an innovative insurance policy, an undergraduate Clark Kent. In all likelihood, and with Lady Fortuna's blessing, E's freshman year will be decidedly ordinary, and you and I will have a wonderfully comfortable and lucrative ride. However, should misfortune befall her fragile constitution, it will be our responsibility, I daresay duty, to avert the treacherous pitfalls that would otherwise lie in waiting.

Fondly,
Michael

Ted sat in the second row of folding chairs at Breathing Easy II, carefully folding a dollar bill into a fighter jet. At his side, a squat, elderly man in a Sergio Tacchini jumpsuit was balancing his hands on the edge of his seat and furiously flexing his jaw. Ted couldn't decide if the man's flinching lips were an involuntary tremor or a rehearsed meditation, but he was amazed that such a still body could have the mouth of a tethered beagle.

"We've got two minutes, so I'm going to pass the basket, and it's Burning Desire time," Ronny P. said.

Ted raised his right hand and splayed his fingers, like he was calling for the ball. He'd been trying to share for the last ten minutes, but he'd been passed over for the meeting's treasurer and a high-school science teacher.

Ronny pointed his finger in Ted's direction. "You," he said, blinking rapidly.

Ted lowered his hand and coughed into his fist. "Ted, alcoholic."

"Hi, Ted."

"I—I didn't think I was going to get called on," Ted said, cracking his knuckles. "I guess I just really need to share. I'm new to the area, for school."

"Welcome," Ronny announced.

"Thanks." Ted nodded. "I should probably just talk about tonight, since I keep spinning it around and around in my head or whatever. It's not a big deal, but I was eating dinner with these three kids from my dorm. Like in the lounge, because one of the girls is from Spain, and she'd cooked all these real Spanish dishes. And so I don't really know any of them very well. I mean, I've seen them around, but it was kind of like a nice gesture for them to invite me, I guess. Well, they were all drinking red wine, which wasn't a huge issue because I was never a wine drinker, and they only offered me once. But halfway through the meal, this crew guy pulls out a tight joint."

The middle-aged woman sitting in front of Ted shook her head gently from side to side. She'd been studiously working a seaside needlepoint all meeting, and she suddenly hugged the plastic grid to her chest.

"I don't know if I panicked or whatever or didn't think it was a big deal, but I didn't say anything. So he sparks it up, and after a couple hits, I knew I had to get out of there. I mean that warm smell, and I wasn't even a big toker. Whatever. I knew I had to leave, 'cause I could like feel the smell, and I said I was going to the head. And ten steps from the room, I just knew I wasn't going back. So I left and started walking over here. I don't know whether I'm overreacting or what, but I can still fucking feel that smoke, like in my sinuses."

Surveying the group, Ted spotted the science teacher nodding his head. They made eye contact, and the teacher alertly raised his hitchhiker's thumb.

"And the thing that pisses me off is that I know they're probably sitting there in the lounge, staring at my full plate of food and talking about what a fucking square I am. How I wouldn't drink their wine, even though I could've drunk the whole bottle by myself in two seconds, and how I was scared of fucking weed. I don't know. I still want to smack that guy and be like, 'Shot for shot, you and me, you fucking lightweight.'

"Yuck." Ted had had two cups of coffee since the meeting started, and he suddenly felt like he was rambling. "So I guess I just really want classes to kick in, and I can't believe I'm saying those words, but maybe everything will sort of settle down. It's just a real shitty time because everybody is going to like fifteen parties a night, and I'm not meeting anybody or whatever. So, thanks for letting me share."

The circle broke into lazy applause, stood up from their chairs, and joined hands. Ronny waited for the sounds of purses and coffee cups and sneakers to settle.

"God," Ronny started.

The meeting echoed Ronny and then began, "Grant me the serenity to accept the things I cannot change, the courage to change the things I can, and the wisdom to know the difference."

With their fingers still laced together, the room pumped their hands to the syllabic count. "Keep coming back. It works, if you work it. So work it, you're worth it."

The elderly man in Sergio Tachini stared up at Ted and stuck his hand straight at Ted's stomach. "Knew a girl in Albuquerque who did college sober. Good man, good man."

"Thank you." Ted collapsed his folding chair and escorted it to the gathering stack in the corner of the room. ·

Outside the First Unitarian Church, Ted watched the crowd racing through cigarettes and rehashing war stories. The Spanish dinner was probably finished by now, but he felt like he couldn't go back to the dorm for another couple of hours. After a few minutes of eavesdropping on a group of Vietnam vets discussing a nearby Internet café, he started down Henry Street.

Ted had already decided he liked walking the streets surrounding the college. The sidewalks were all paved with red brick or cobblestone, and most of the houses were manicured landmark Colonials. At night, if nobody else was around, he found himself pretending it was two hundred years earlier.

As Ted passed the electric-candlelit windows of an olive two-story, he heard the rapid clatter of heels on stone. Fifty feet in front of him, the shaded figure of a woman emerged from the line of sleeping Colonials. He watched her scan the empty sidewalk in both directions and then start toward him.

The high beams of a turning Saab blinded Ted for a second,

and when his pupils rebalanced, he recognized the serrated out-lines of Erica's curly hair. He quickly considered making a sharp right downhill. Then he remembered the headlights.

Twenty feet from her, Ted realized it was a Saturday night, and he was dressed in ripped jeans and a VARSITY sweatshirt. Stuffing his hands in his jeans pockets, he cycled frantically through his night's story.

"Hey, insomniac," Erica said, firmly crossing her arms over her gray silk halter. She couldn't decide if Ted was lost or just hang-ing out on the corner. "What's going on?"

Ted shrugged, waiting for her to take the final three steps that separated them. "Not much."

"I'm so fucking pissed off."

Inhaling the musty smell of cheap beer, Ted tried to gauge how drunk she was. "Are you okay?"

"No, I'm not fucking okay," Erica half-shouted, and swung her purse onto her shoulder. She didn't mean to raise her voice, but it felt good.

"What—"

"We go to a school filled with assholes."

Erica was wobbly and slightly slurring, but Ted could tell she didn't need to work to get there. He guessed she'd had two or three beers. "What happened?"

"Nothing," she said, loosely shaking her head. "Everything. But I want to keep walking." She pointed past Ted's shoulder, and he instinctively turned.

"I guess I could probably use the fresh air."

"Good. The point is that the fraternity system should be abol-ished." Erica kicked a felled branch out of their way and reached into her purse. "It's like everybody's willing to look the other way and let these guys bring back the Middle fucking Ages."

"Did you go to that Sigma Chi thing tonight?"

"Yes, I went to *that party*," she said, exasperated.

"I didn't go," he said, quickly trying to disassociate himself.

"Well, here's what you'd have seen. Dozens and dozens of girls selling themselves to those fucking frat bastards for some stupid Mardi Gras beads." Erica removed a packet of tissues from her purse and wiped her lips. She wanted to believe she'd put her face on for herself, but she knew it wasn't true.

Ted listened to the dead leaves drifting across the bricks as he searched desperately for a response. "My roommate went, I think."

"You live with James Zachary, right?"

"Yeah, short guy," Ted said, enjoying the sound of it.

"That kid should be shot at first light," Erica declared. "Our fathers are friends, and he's the fucking embodiment of every stupid, dirty-white-hat, WASPy, kind-of-rich, boarding-school, Dave-Matthews-Band-listening, alcoholic idiot."

Ted turned to Erica and grinned, waiting to see if she was finished. "I don't think I understood what you just said, but you sound right."

"I am right, and I'll tell you what else. He told me you're a Jesus freak."

"What?" Ted suddenly felt like walking over to Sigma Chi and dragging James out onto the quad. He'd already decided that James was the kind of kid you only had to hit once.

"Because you don't go out with him and his idiot friends." Erica tossed the used tissue over her shoulder like spilled salt. She wasn't sure why, but she needed Ted to hate James as much as she did.

Ted's hand darted out and caught the tissue at its vertex. He stuffed it in the back pocket of his jeans behind his meeting book. "We probably haven't spent more than ten minutes together."

"I told him you were an enigma," Erica said, impressed by Ted's quickness.

"Fucking asshole," he whispered.

"Oh, don't let that pathetic piece of shit get under your skin," Erica cried into the breeze. Her heels were miraculously gliding across the chipped brick, and for the first time all night, she was enjoying her beer buzz.

"If—"

"*Normal* is sitting up there in that frat house. So you can consider yourself saved not to be that."

"Whatever," Ted said. "Fuck 'em."

"That's right. Fuck 'em all."

"So where are we walking?"

"To whatever that mini-mart is on Sheldon," Erica said, pretending to forget the name Kwik-Mart.

"Okay."

"They've got cherry slushies," Erica explained. "I think I'm addicted to them."

"Sounds dangerous."

"And I'm feeling pretty strung out right now."

"You should probably check out a Twelve-Step group."

Erica looked over at Ted, surprised by his joke. "So why don't you go out with everybody?"

"I don't know. I'm not much of a party guy, I guess."

Erica tilted her chin playfully, weighing his answer. "We're going to need a judge's ruling on that," she said in a broadcaster's voice.

"It's not a judgment thing, I swear," Ted said anxiously. "I think I just have weird habits."

"Huh. I figured you for one of those shy genius types," Erica lied.

"How?" Ted asked, surprised.

"Well, you're not a dork, 'cause I can just tell that. And you're not a jock, 'cause you don't practice with any of the teams. And—"

"But why do I have to be anything?" Ted said defensively.

"Relax, it's just a game. Besides, I meant it as a compliment. Scout's honor."

Erica and Ted turned onto Sheldon Street. Down the block, the fluorescent panels of the Kwik-Mart lit the faces of loitering students and refracted off windshields.

"So what would you say you are?" Ted asked. "I mean, if you have to be something."

Erica wrapped her arms around her chest and rubbed her biceps. She'd spent hours revising her title with Laura, but she wanted the suspense. "Postfeminist with a sweet tooth."

Ted smiled. "For slushies?"

"Yeah."

"I think I get the *feminist* part, but what does the *post* mean?"

"What does it mean? What does it mean?" Erica muttered. "It means that half the girls at this school think they're feminists, even though they're wearing Mardi Gras beads and running around conforming to the same ridiculous stereotypes."

"So that's not you?"

"No, that's not me," Erica declared.

"Then I'm probably the quiet ex-jock," Ted said, pausing on each word.

"That's got a ring to it."

"Thanks."

"Quiet ex-jock who doesn't like parties," Erica read like she was trying out a newspaper headline.

Ted nodded and pulled at the door to the Kwik-Mart. It didn't budge. He looked down, read the handle, and pushed the door open. "Yeah, I guess that, too."

"What sport *did* you play?" Erica walked over to the self-serve kegs of slushies and pumped the cherry handle.

"Basketball." Ted grabbed a bottle of Mountain Dew from the refrigerator display case. He could feel the coffee caffeine draining out of his bloodstream, and he didn't want to crash yet.

Erica carefully topped off her sixteen-ounce plastic cup and then ran her tongue around the lip of the container. "Were you any good?" she asked, waiting for the cool buzz.

"Yeah." Ted nodded, twisted the cap off his soda, and took a short sip. "Better at that than anything else."

Erica walked up to the cashier's counter and nodded hello to the young clerk. The clerk was wearing an ocean-blue vest with a Dunkin' Donuts visor slanted to the side, and Ted recognized his begrudging greeting.

Sliding her slushie across the countertop, Erica placed her fingers over the top of Ted's soda and lifted it from his grip. "My treat," she said, pulling a fan of singles from her purse. "For the escort."

Ted suddenly wanted to rip the dollar bills from Erica's hand and shred them to pieces. Pressing his palm to his chest, he begged his stomach to save him from throwing up in the middle of the Kwik-Mart.

"And why the *ex*-jock?" Erica asked, wondering how far she was from The Tavern Bar. If she invited Ted to come with her, she knew she couldn't finish the entire slushie in front of him.

Ted opened his mouth, unsure if his body was planning to speak or breathe or puke. "Wrecked my knee."

"That sucks." As they walked toward the exit, Erica searched Ted's grimace and decided it was a jagged memory.

"Yeah."

Erica stepped outside and sipped her slushie. "I think I'm going to go meet up with Lindsey at The Tavern." The chipped ice stung her teeth, and she smiled involuntarily at Ted. "You feel like checking it out?"

"I think I'm probably going to crash."

"This isn't a party," she said, enjoying her numbed lips.

Ted shrugged and tried to smile back. "I'm cool. Thanks for the walk, though."

"Well, if you change your mind, let me give you my cell," Erica said casually, suddenly realizing she must be drunk.

"Cool." He reached for his cell phone. "Okay."

"917-555-7254," Erica recited, watching Ted's thumb stab each button. It was the first time she'd given her number to a guy at school, but she couldn't decide if this really counted. "'Cause I'm going to drag you out one of these night."

"If you say so."

She rolled her eyes and gave Ted a short wave. "Well, I'll see you back at the dorm."

"Cool." Ted turned his back on Erica and the Kwik-Mart and hit SAVE.

Date: Monday, 15 Sep 11:56:21
From: TedFIN@Highsmith.com
To: MichaelFIN@Highsmith.com

No news here. I ran into E. on B. street Saturday night at around eleven. She'd just left a frat party and she was a little bit tipsy. I don't think she likes the frat scene at school but I don't blame her because most of those people kind of suck. We walked to the mini-mart and talked about the party and guys in our unit. Random stuff mostly. Then she went to meet up with some people I don't know at a bar and I headed back to the dorm. This was only the second time we've talked but she seems like she's fitting in here better than I am. Also I wasn't sure what you meant by me being a Clark Kent. If I see E. doing something bad what can I do about it? C. never said what would happen or anything and I guess I'd like to know.

T.

Date: Monday, 15 Sep 17:29:41
From: MichaelFIN@Highsmith.com
To: TedFIN@Highsmith.com

Cheers,

I'm very pleased to hear that E's enjoying an active social life and I too share your collective disdain for hierarchical Nouveau-Wasp culture. Perhaps it's simply an excuse for strapping young men to publicly paddle one another.

Separately, I spoke with C about our various contingency plans for E and, unfortunately, he forbade me from sharing them with you. However, I can say that in the event E should resume her destructive behaviors, E would be discreetly withdrawn from the university and placed on indefinite leave. You would be released from your current responsibilities, free to pursue a degree at your leisure. Again, let me assure you, your daily collegiate life would continue unchanged.

Discreetly,
Michael

Date: Monday, 15 Sep 21:05:43
From: TedFIN@Highsmith.com
To: MichaelFIN@Highsmith.com

I know I'm not an expert on stuff like this but I think you guys are kind of overreacting. I mean isn't there some way for E. to get help at school without all of that drama. Cause if you pull her out of school just like that she's going to be really furious and I know that's not going to help her try and beat this thing. One of the backup guys on my team got sober and he was always talking about how he was the only person who could make the decision to get straight or whatever. I know you guys probably have everything all figured out to the last details but I thought you might want to know my opinion since I see her every day.
T.

Date: Tuesday, 16 Sep 02:29:41
From: MichaelFIN@Highsmith.com
To: TedFIN@Highsmith.com

Cheers,

In the words of my countryman, Lord Alfred Tennyson, and his Light Brigade,
Theirs not to make reply,
Theirs not to reason why,
Theirs but to do and die.

Poetically,
Michael

Erica couldn't decide how long her eyes had been open. She wanted to believe that her eyelids had just blinked awake, but she felt as if she'd been staring at the ceiling for the last hour, waiting for the rest of her body to come to. The next thought pulsed lazily through her brain: She wasn't in her own bed. Her breathing quickened. She started to sit up. The web of muscles in her neck sent an aching shudder down her spine, and she gave up on the idea of moving.

Sinking back into her pillow, Erica realized her tongue was sealed to the roof of her mouth. All of the saliva had been vacuumed from her gums, and she could smell stale bourbon in her clogged sinuses. Erica scanned the room for something to drink. She was covered to her collarbone with a wool blanket, and at the foot of the bed, she recognized the shape and color of her toes. She knew they were her feet, but something about their distant stillness made her wonder whether somebody had forged a wax duplicate.

Studying the curved skin of her pinkie toe, Erica felt a swell of panic. She had no idea if she was clothed. With the tips of her fingers, she lifted the edge of the blanket and stared down at her pale breasts and stomach. Her hands started to shake, and she raised the blanket until she could see the elastic rim of her underwear. She suddenly wanted to yell for help, but she didn't even know where she was.

Dropping the blanket back to her chest, Erica massaged her dry eyes with her palms. Her head felt like it was filled with sand, and she couldn't remember taking off her shirt or her jeans or even where they were. She looked over at the varnished oak bed on the opposite side of the room. From her low angle, she could see mounds of dark blue quilting resting on the mattress, but she couldn't make out the shape of a body.

Erica heard a rush of air behind her and then a violent sneeze. A shiver of nausea swept through her body like the first sign of flu. She rolled over on the bed and stared at James Zachary. His eyes were still closed, and she watched a snot bubble inflate and burst against his cheeks. Fragments from the night before flickered on the surface of Erica's memory like an out-of-control slide show: two cans of MGD balanced on top of each other, a half-eaten garlic knot, a pack of Parliaments. She remembered leaning against the damp brick wall of Billiard Bar, and then she realized she was crying.

Pooling tears warmed the bridge of her nose and streaked down her cheekbones. Closing her eyes, Erica begged her thoughts to slow down.

"Hey," a voice whispered.

Erica flinched to her right and spotted Ted at the edge of his bed. The blue quilt was now wrapped around his waist like a towel, and his face and chest were lying against the cover sheet.

"You okay?" Ted asked. It had been one hundred and twenty-seven days since his last drink, but he could still feel the stiffness of a hangover's first breath.

Erica slowly shook her head, scolding herself to stop crying. She lifted the blanket to the tip of her chin.

Ted wiped his bangs from his forehead and remembered the way he used to leave a thirty-two-ounce water bottle and a pair of Tylenols by his nightstand. It was the first thing he did every morning. "Can I do anything?"

"Quiet." She nodded at James.

"He sleeps like the dead," Ted said. "Probably better than that when he's hung over."

Erica debated wrapping the blanket around her body and scurrying back to her room, but she couldn't be sure the hallway was empty. If somebody spotted her, she knew she'd have to pack up and head back to New York.

"I must look pretty stupid right now," Erica muttered. "After everything I said the other night."

"I—"

"It's because of these fucking pills I'm taking," she said, swallowing a surge of tears. Doctor Rudas had warned her not to drink on Prozac, and in the last thirty seconds she'd decided that the medication had scrambled her memory.

"You don't need to be embarrassed around me, I don't think." Ted tallied seven empty cans of Milwaukee's Best on James's nightstand: three flattened, two overturned, and two still standing. He hated counting James's empties every morning, but he couldn't help it.

"Too late," Erica whispered. "Can you—"

"I mean, I've probably done a lot crazier things from drinking and stuff."

"Wanna bet?" Erica said angrily. She pressed her fingers to her eyelashes and skimmed the moisture. "You're a fucking Boy Scout, right?"

Sitting up in bed, Ted leaned against the wall. "I used to piss myself. Like in front of people when I was passed out."

"Yeah?" All she could think about was finding her shirt.

"Right in the middle of parties and stuff. I think people thought I was crazy."

James's side of the floor was littered with piles of clothes, sneakers, splayed textbooks, and Erica scanned the clutter. "Sounds pretty crazy to me," she said absently.

"I even—"

James let out a long, bored yawn and lazily rubbed his hip.

"Do you know where my clothes are?" Erica asked urgently.

Hearing the quiet tremble in her voice, Ted slid to the end of his bed and grabbed his warm-up pants off the bedpost. He planted his good leg on the carpet and started searching through James's mess. Pulling out James's desk chair, he knocked over his dirty laundry pile.

"I—" Ted hesitated, watching Erica's lips slowly mouth the word *fuck*. "Maybe I could go grab your bathrobe?"

Erica nodded. "It's on my door hook."

"Okay."

"But," she said, reaching out to Ted, "if my roommate's there, just pretend like you're looking for me or something. Okay?"

"Got it." Ted reached over to his desk chair and grabbed his dirty V-neck. Edging open the door, he smiled nervously back at Erica and then slid into the hallway.

Erica listened to the soft click of the doorknob and squeezed her eyes shut. She couldn't understand how she deserved this. She might hate herself some mornings, but she refused to believe that cosmic forces hated her, too. And yet, she was lying here trapped. She suddenly wished Ted hadn't left. As long as someone was there, talking to her, she felt like she could tread water.

The door swung back open, and Erica decided that if it wasn't Ted, if it was some random person she'd never met before, she was going to be back in the city by sundown. Her father and Doctor Rudas would laugh at her, but she didn't care.

Ted slipped through the doorway, the white bathrobe draped over his forearm like a busboy. "I'm . . ." His voice faded as he debated where to leave the robe. He considered handing it to Erica, but he worried about approaching her. He could see how mortified she was, and he guessed it would be easier for her if he just dropped the bathrobe to the floor and left.

Ted balanced the robe on the back of James's desk chair. "I

guess I'm just going to leave it here. I'll be outside and . . . okay," he said, inching away from her. Spinning around, he stepped back through the doorway.

Erica clutched the blanket to her chest, leaned forward, and dragged the robe across the bedding. Swinging her legs to the floor, she felt the fall air tickle her goose bumps. She double-checked James. He was crouched in the fetal position, hands locked together, resting between his thighs. She let go of the blanket and quickly wrapped herself in terry cloth.

Kicking over James's monogrammed towels, Erica found her wrinkled jeans and balled-up shirt. She slid her clothes into her robe and tightened the belt. Erica spotted her black leather purse on James's desk. Everything was still there: money, cell phone, eyeliner, lip gloss, tissues. At the bottom of her purse, she found three Sour Apple Blow-Pop wrappers. She couldn't remember buying them, or even liking Sour Apple, but she'd obviously had a craving.

Erica caught her reflection in the flip side of a loose CD. Eyeliner was streaked across the top of her cheeks, and she wondered if Ted thought she looked like a raccoon. Grabbing her tissues, she lifted a half-empty bottle of Poland Spring from James's blotter. She covered the top of the water bottle with a handful of tissues and flipped it upside down. She wasn't sure why, but she couldn't leave their room without cleaning her face. She needed to see the watery ink.

Erica dropped the dirty tissues on top of James's Mercedes key ring, tiptoed across the room, and delicately turned the doorknob. Stepping into the hallway, she saw Ted coming out of the bathroom four doors down. He lowered his glance to the carpet.

"Do you want to borrow that CD?" Erica asked, nodding toward her room.

"Yeah. Cool," Ted added naturally.

Walking through the stairwell, Erica crossed over to her side of the hallway. She held her door open for Ted, and he stepped tentatively into the middle of the room. Erica sat down on the edge of her racing-green duvet and tossed the dirty clothes into her hamper.

"Look, I just wanted to thank you," Erica began, reaching for an old can of Fresca. She swallowed a mouthful of sour water.

Ted leaned against Maisy's desk. "No problem."

"You can sit on Maisy's bed. I'm sure she wouldn't mind."

Ted propped Maisy's teddy bears against the wall. "Thanks."

"I don't know how to ask this," Erica said, pausing. "I mean I've never had to ask it before, so I guess I'll just come right out and ask it or whatever. Did you see us come in last night?"

Ted ran his fingers along the grooves in Maisy's quilt. "You mean you and James?" he said, realizing she'd blacked out. Ted had blacked out dozens of times, but he always remembered the first. He'd waked up on the floor of Drew's bedroom, surrounded by dozens of stacks of nickels and dimes. Apparently, he'd spent the night organizing Drew's fishbowl of change.

"Yeah," Erica said, irritated. She knew he was stalling.

"I probably woke up for a few seconds, I guess."

"Well?"

"I mean, what do you want to know?" Ted asked, trying to hide from her stare. The Magritte poster above her bed was an enormous eye with a cloudy-sky iris, and Ted couldn't help but feel like the poster was studying him as well.

"What happened? Did we hook up, nothing, what?"

"I wouldn't say it was a hookup. I mean, I think you pretty much undressed yourself. You know, to sleep and stuff."

"Oh, fuck," Erica mumbled. She pictured James and Ted's

squinting eyes combing the awkward surfaces of her body, the fine black hairs resting below her belly button, the translucent blue vein that zigzagged along her left thigh, a pair of pimples on her right shoulder blade. Erica suddenly wanted to crawl into her bed and sleep away the next twenty-four hours.

"I guess you guys were both pretty gone when you came in, and you . . . and I watched you guys both kind of strip down or whatever. I mean, not like watched, watched," Ted said softly. "But I saw."

"So we didn't hook up?" Erica asked hopefully.

"Not really, no."

"What do you mean, 'Not really'?"

"Well," Ted said hesitantly. "I think James kind of kissed your shoulder for a while. Like while you were falling asleep. Your right shoulder."

Erica swallowed a jolt of anxiety. "Just my shoulder?"

"I guess it was probably more like sucking on your shoulder or something."

"What?" Erica pulled at the collar of her bathrobe and exposed her slightly reddened shoulder muscle. The scattered flush reminded her of a sloppy hickey, but she couldn't see any teeth marks.

"Almost like nursing or something," Ted finished. "I bet he doesn't even remember any of it."

"What a fucking psycho!"

"I'm sure he won't remember it," Ted added. "I mean, his eyes were closed, and he never seems to remember the end of his night anyway."

"And then nothing else?" Erica asked, slightly relieved. She couldn't decide if this was wonderful or tragic news.

"That was it, I think."

"So this isn't so bad?" Erica promised herself that in ten minutes she'd be in a scalding shower. After that, she'd find a greasy breakfast to cut the hangover.

"No."

"Good."

Ted shrugged and cracked his knuckles.

"So you don't think I'm a total slut?" Erica asked, half jokingly.

"No," Ted said, shaking his head. "Not at all."

"Good. Me neither," Erica declared. If she could say it out loud, then she decided she probably believed it.

Erica plucked her stereo remote off the bedside table and hit PLAY. She'd been listening to Björk's *Debut* while she was getting ready last night, and she'd paused the disc halfway through "Venus As a Boy."

"So you don't think James will even remember?" Erica said.

"That's my guess."

"Can you let me know? I mean, when he wakes up, can you just let me know if he mentions anything?"

"Yeah."

"I'd really appreciate that." Erica thought about calling Laura, but she wasn't ready to rehash everything.

"No problem."

"I know you probably have your own social bullshit to deal with and stuff."

"Not really," Ted muttered.

"Well, then, I guess you're lucky."

"I guess."

Erica's door swung open, and Maisy danced into the room in a Champion hooded sweatshirt and navy sweatpants. A little over five feet, she had her curly red hair up in a tight ponytail, and her cheeks were littered with pin-sized freckles.

Maisy smiled and scattered her freckles. "Hey, guys," she erupted, tossing her meal card onto her desk. "How goes?"

"Not bad," Erica said, wondering what her Roman Catholic roommate thought of her lounging around in front of Ted.

Ted slid off Maisy's bed and onto the floor, and Maisy playfully inspected his tall frame. "Maisy Landrigan," she said, extending her hand.

"You guys haven't met?" Erica asked, surprised.

Ted shook her small palm. "Ted York."

Maisy pressed her hand to her stomach, stuck out her tongue, and groaned. "Team breakfasts are going to kill me—"

"Ted lives across the hall," Erica interrupted.

"Oh, right," Maisy said, grinning.

"Well, I should get going." Ted tapped his wrist and turned to Erica. "But I'll let you know about that CD."

Erica nodded. "Cool."

Ted stepped around Maisy.

"Come back soon," Maisy chimed.

He forced a smile and bowed through the doorway. "Thanks."

Maisy walked quickly over to the door and edged it closed. Then she skipped back to her bed and dove onto her mattress. "What are you doing with Creepy Cutie?" she asked.

"Wh-what?" Erica stuttered.

"Ted whatever his name is."

"No, what'd you call him?"

Maisy rolled her eyes and then folded her legs into the lotus position. "Oh, it's this nickname Julia and Eve made up for him. You know, those two girls on the third floor."

"He's not creepy."

"Oh, come on. He doesn't talk to anybody. He doesn't go out. And Keith saw him talking with these two flamers outside that church on Grove Street."

"I guess he's shy," Erica offered.

Maisy straightened her legs and pointed her toes at the ceiling. "He's gorgeous, is what he is."

"Well, he's not one of those guys who acts like he is," Erica said, picturing Ted's nervous Granny Smith eyes.

"Like Dennis Quaid gorgeous."

"I guess something like that."

"So what's he like?"

Erica tried to remember their conversations in the lounge and on the way to the Kwik-Mart. "He's really . . ." She paused. "He's really gentle."

Maisy laughed. "See, I told you he was weird."

Date: Wednesday, 17 Sep 14:13:49
From: MichaelFIN@Highsmith.com
To: TedFIN@Highsmith.com

Cheers,

Please forgive my foul mood. Having just burnt my second bag of Newman's Own Microwave Popcorn, I'm debating waging consumer warfare against their self-destructive product line.

With a few moments to myself this evening, I wanted to draw your attention to E's erratic sleeping schedule. E's father has been kind enough to provide me with access to her cell phone account, and her recent calling patterns are cause for moderate concern. Sunday through Tuesday, E was on her cell with her best friend L from 2:03 am - 3:35 am, 2:47 am - 4:28 am, and 2:16 am - 4:01 am, successively. It's probably nothing more than her acclimation process, but I was hoping you might tune your proverbial antenna onto her late-night activity. Obviously, I will continue to monitor her account, and I will let you know if this pattern arrests itself.

Buttery,
Michael

Date: Wednesday, 17 Sep 18:56:21
From: TedFIN@Highsmith.com
To: MichaelFIN@Highsmith.com

Huh. That kind of surprises me. I go to the bathroom a couple times a night usually because I'm a real light sleeper and I've never seen E. on her cell. We talked in the lounge that one time but I haven't seen her around again late night. I guess it's possible that E.'s friend is waking her up in bed and then E. just chats from there. Right? Otherwise I feel like I would've spotted her. I'll keep an eye out.
T.

---

ep149846: well i fucking hate taking it
DrMTRudas: Erica, I hear what you're saying, but I sincerely believe it's unreasonable to blame your blackout on Prozac.
ep149846: thanks for telling me how my body works doc . . . and you're hanging your rook out to dry
DrMTRudas: Might it simply be a case of excessive college drinking, unrelated to your medication? And I lost that piece three moves ago.
ep149846: whatever . . . it doesn't work and it's making me balloon

DrMTRudas: Give it time. You've only been at a full dose for one month.

ep149846: why should i

DrMTRudas: Because I want to help you. Because I truly feel this medication could be beneficial.

ep149846: do these drug companies give you a cut . . . bye-bye mr rook

DrMTRudas: Erica, your decision to take or not take a psycho-pharmaceutical has absolutely zero financial impact on me. I cannot stress it enough: I have your best interests at heart.

ep149846: fine

DrMTRudas: I WANT YOU TO BE WONDERFULLY HAPPY, ERICA!!!

ep149846: i said fine . . . and EASY ON THE CAPS

DrMTRudas: Sorry. Can I ask you a question about the black-out?

ep149846: fire away

DrMTRudas: Did something happen that you now regret?

ep149846: what makes you think that

DrMTRudas: Call it professional intuition.

ep149846: yes

DrMTRudas: Would you like to tell me about it?

ep149846: no

DrMTRudas: Okay.

***checkmate

ep149846: well played doc

DrMTRudas: You're still up 7-5. One more? We have a few minutes left in our hour.

ep149846: i sort of hooked up with this guy james . . . and he's a total fucking asshole

DrMTRudas: I see. I assume that's frustrating for you.

ep149846: yeah

DrMTRudas: How are you feeling about it?
ep149846: time's up . . . see you later

Date: Thursday, 18 Sep 16:13:49
From: MichaelFIN@Highsmith.com
To: TedFIN@Highsmith.com

Cheers,

Seeing as how you were wide awake on two of the three nights and
similarly engaged in long distance cell phone conversations, I hoped
you might be able to offer more considered insight. (N.B. To answer
that nagging question, I should remind you that information, like
everything else in this world, always has its price.) However, since you
were otherwise occupied, let me inform you that E did not spend the
lengths of her phone calls burrowed underneath a tent of blankets. In
fact, on two of these evenings, at the approximate midpoint of her
call, she withdrew ten dollars from the aforementioned mini-mart
ATM. You are my eyes and ears, Theodore, and I expect great things
from you. Please, stay focused.

Eagerly,
Michael

Date: Friday, 19 Sep 13:09:55
From: TedFIN@Highsmith.com
To: MichaelFIN@Highsmith.com

How the hell do you know all this stuff? Are you following her
around? Is someone else? I know you make the rules but I wish I

didn't feel like people were sneaking around on me. It really creeps me out to be honest with you. We may not be playing the same position but we're on the same team right? I still don't have any info on these walks you say E.'s taking except maybe about why she's walking to the mini-mart. She loves cherry slushies. Not that it matters in the first place.

T.

DrMTRudas: Yo!

ep149846: you're not funny

DrMTRudas: Sorry. How are you doing today?

ep149846: i'm in a shitty fucking mood thank you

DrMTRudas: Anything in particular?

ep149846: same shit from before . . . every time i see james i want to punch him in the fucking face

DrMTRudas: I see. That's tough.

ep149846: yup

DrMTRudas: How are you doing with your meals?

ep149846: fine

DrMTRudas: What does fine mean?

ep149846: fine means fine

DrMTRudas: I know fine means fine, but will you tell me what else fine means?

ep149846: fine means i'm not fucking perfect and nobody else is

DrMTRudas: I don't expect you or me or anybody to be perfect, Erica. My goal is progress.

ep149846: well it was one meal and it just happened

DrMTRudas: Just happened?

ep149846: as in i didn't intend for it to happen . . . i just crossed a line when I was out to lunch yesterday and that was it

DrMTRudas: I understand. I guess one could make a distinction between premeditated and unintended.

ep149846: yup . . . this morning was pretty fucking intended

DrMTRudas: I see. Given your cyclical history, are you concerned that this will be the beginning of a downward trend?

ep149846: my only concern is that you'll keep bugging me about it

DrMTRudas: Erica, I think this is something we need to take very seriously.

ep149846: i've been a saint for weeks okay

DrMTRudas: Do you think the incident with James is making things more difficult?

ep149846: i think i'm doing the best i can and you should shut the fuck up

DrMTRudas: Fair enough. Do you feel like playing a game of chess? I was practicing over the weekend with a colleague.

ep149846: i can hardly wait

"So classes are going good?" Ted's father asked.

Ted had been coiling circles in the margins of his accounting textbook for the last five minutes of their phone conversation. "Yeah. They're fine, I think," he said, tossing his pen into the book.

"And how you doing with meetings?"

"Good." Ted slid his *Alcoholics Anonymous* Big Book off his bookshelf and dropped it onto the desk. "I'm going to one in a bit."

"And you're talking with Paul a bunch?"

"Every couple nights. He doesn't get home till late."

"He's a solid guy," Ted's father declared.

"All he does is lecture me."

"Maybe that's what you need."

Ted's doorknob clicked, and he spun around in his chair. Erica leaned her torso through the door frame.

"Hey, can I call you back?" Ted asked, waving Erica inside.

"We'll talk tomorrow."

"Okay," Ted whispered. "Bye."

"Hey," Erica began. She'd put on her jean jacket, and after a short mirror debate, she'd decided to fasten only the bottom two buttons. One button bowed the jacket into an enormous denim blouse, and three buttons focused her eyes on her hips. "You didn't need to—"

"It was just my dad," Ted interrupted.

"Any word from you-know-who?" Erica asked hesitantly, nodding toward James's bed.

Ted wiggled his hand. "He knows a girl crashed on his bed, but he thinks it's somebody named Scarlet. At least, that's what he was saying on the phone."

"She lives on the fourth floor," Erica said, grinning. "I think she walked home with us from the bar."

"Yeah." Ted laughed. "He sounded pretty nervous about calling her up."

"Perfect."

"Not bad," he agreed.

"Well, I was thinking about walking over to the Comm to get a cup of coffee. You want to take a break?" Erica had rehearsed the offer a half-dozen times in her room, and she suddenly felt like she was reading off a teleprompter. "Or something," she improvised.

Ted instinctively checked his watch. He had thirty minutes until the Sober Living Big Book meeting, and it was at least a ten-minute walk. "I probably—"

"No need to explain," Erica said as casually as she could. She promptly placed her hand back on the doorknob.

"No, I just need to get to the library before it closes."

"The Sciences?"

Ted quickly recalculated his route to the Second Baptist Church. "Yeah."

"Cool. Well, I'll walk halfway with you."

"Cool," Ted repeated. "Let me get a sweater."

Staring at the bottom drawer of his dresser, Ted debated whether or not or he could get away with grabbing the Big Book off his desk. He'd replaced the dust jacket with the one from his mother's copy of *The Sheltering Sky,* but he worried that Erica would start asking him questions about the novel or the author. Ted picked a brown cable-knit and then decided to leave the Big Book behind. He could always read along with somebody.

Pulling the sweater over his head, Ted turned around to face Erica. She was sitting on the edge of his desk chair, looking down at his copy of *Principles of Financial Accounting.*

"I don't know how you can read this stuff," Erica said.

"It's not so bad."

She absently flipped the page. "What else are you taking?"

"Two math courses—"

"Yuck," Erica groaned, and playfully stuck out her tongue. She'd meticulously brushed her teeth fifteen minutes earlier, and the dorm air stung her taste buds.

"What?" Ted knew she was kidding, but he'd spent so many hours debating his courses that it annoyed him.

"Too many numbers."

"I like numbers," Ted declared, wondering if it sounded stupid.

"You should check out Intro Music Theory. It's the best class I'm taking."

"I think I'd probably be pretty terrible at that."

"You'll never know until you try," Erica teased.

"But what's a music course going to prepare me to actually do?"

"Anything in music. Musician, producer, concert promoter, booking agent." Erica ran her finger across the mini-bookshelf above Ted's desk, her nail tripping from *Merriam-Webster's Collegiate Dictionary* to *The Official NBA Basketball Encyclopedia* to *Roget's 21st Century Thesaurus*. Then she reached across his desk and brushed the dust jacket of *The Sheltering Sky*.

"Those jobs aren't for people like us," Ted said, searching desperately for a segue away from his desk.

"Speak for yourself. I'm starting my own record label."

"For real?" Ted stepped toward the doorway, hoping she'd follow. He couldn't decide what he was more terrified of, Erica simply knowing or having to find the words to explain why he went to AA meetings.

Erica pressed her thumb against *The Sheltering Sky* cover. "You know this is a great novel." She'd figured Ted for a Tom Clancy or John Grisham fan.

"You want to get going?" he asked, anxiously nodding toward the hallway. He was suddenly convinced Erica would gossip the news across the entire dorm.

"Which edition is this?" She tilted the spine toward her. "It looks really thick."

Swinging open the door, Ted waved her hastily outside. "Time to go—"

"Chill," Erica said, irritated. She'd wanted to thank him for Wednesday morning, but she wasn't going to let herself be badgered.

Ted considered grabbing the book from her hand, but he didn't want to frighten her. "We need to leave. . . ."

"No need to spaz." Erica tossed the Big Book back onto the desk, stood up, and nervously brushed the front of her jeans. "On second thought," she said, walking past Ted and into the hallway, "I think I'm going to wait a bit on the Comm." Spinning away from him, she walked back to her room.

Ted leaned against the width of his door and felt his stomach cramp. He couldn't understand how he'd misplayed the situation so terribly. Outside of meetings, Erica was the one person he'd had a real conversation with, even if he knew he didn't deserve her trust.

Ted debated calling his father back, but he was too embarrassed to retell the scene. If he went to the Big Book meeting, he knew he'd spend the hour replaying those awkward sixty seconds. Then he considered apologizing. But every explanation he imagined made him seem even stranger. Closing his eyes, he knocked his forehead against the metal door frame.

Ted started walking toward the staircase, hesitated at the first down step, and then found himself on Erica's side of the hallway. He could see the door to her room was slightly ajar, and he instantly felt like kicking the door open and accusing her of snooping. He never picked through people's stuff, and he was convinced that only a spoiled New York City girl would have the nerve to walk all over his privacy.

Standing in front of Erica's door, Ted knocked loudly on her purple name placard. He wanted the steady rap of his knuckles to introduce his seriousness, but there was no response. Opening her door halfway, he saw Erica lying on her back in the middle of her bed. She was staring straight up at the chalk ceiling tiles, and her palms were resting at her sides, like she was on a gurney. He took a step inside and closed the door behind him. She didn't flinch.

Ted opened his mouth, prepared to ask why she'd ignored his knock, but he was struck by Erica's steady, rhythmic breathing. He'd imagined her on the phone, rambling through some exaggerated version of his outburst. Instead, she looked like she was meditating. Four weeks earlier, Paul had driven Ted to an 11th Step Meditation meeting, and he remembered the way the chairperson also seemed to hyperventilate in slow motion.

Erica snapped her head to the side and glared at Ted. He knew he was supposed to say something, but he hadn't expected to find her lying peacefully on her bed.

"I'm an alcoholic," Ted said as the gravity of habit whipped him through his most routine syllables.

Erica sat up on her elbows, startled, and furrowed her brow. Ted watched mutely as she pushed away thick strands of black curls from her ear and popped out a white earbud.

"Sorry?" She'd wrapped herself around Billie Holiday's "Summertime," and she didn't know how long Ted had been standing there.

Ted froze. He still wasn't sure why he'd confessed, but he'd felt a swell of nervous relief blurting it out. "Can you keep a secret?" he asked.

Erica unplugged the other earbud and crossed her legs. "What kind of secret?"

"A personal secret, I guess."

"About you?" Erica asked, wishing he'd left her door open.

"Yeah," Ted said.

"As long as it only affects you, sure."

"'Cause if I tell you, and you tell other people, it could sort of be really bad for me, even if they don't know me. I mean, people have a lot of prejudices and things."

"What is it?"

"I'm an alcoholic," Ted said. "I mean, I think I might be."

Erica squinted at Ted. "What are you talking about?"

He sat down on Maisy's desk chair and gripped the seat cushion. "Well, I've been going to these meetings for the last couple months and—"

"AA meetings?" On Erica's second day in East Hampton Memorial Hospital, she'd wandered into an empty conference room with the Twelve Steps and Twelve Traditions hanging shades. She remembered looking through a fanned display of gray pamphlets and a wicker bowl of plastic silver dollars, wondering how anyone could find salvation in a Cracker Jack toy.

Ted nodded. "Yeah."

"But I've never even seen you drink."

"Well, that's sort of the point," Ted said, smiling. "I mean—"

"Sorry." Erica tugged at her sleeves. "That was stupid."

"I don't know," Ted continued. "I guess I just wanted to say that the book you were looking at was an AA book. Which is kind of why I spazzed or whatever back there."

Erica tilted her head and wrinkled her nose. "Why do you guys read Paul Bowles?"

"No. That was just the dust jacket," Ted said, grinning with relief. "I probably shouldn't have left my Big Book out in the first place."

"That's okay."

"So . . ." Ted cracked his teeth together. "You probably think I'm out of my mind."

Watching Ted's shy eyes, Erica suddenly felt like giving him a hug, but she didn't want to embarrass him. "I think you're one of the bravest people I've met in a long time, Ted."

"Thanks, but I think my life's kind of fallen to pieces."

"Doesn't take much to rip us into pieces," Erica said, humming Tori Amos's piano in "Little Earthquakes."

"But you're not angry at me or anything?" Ted slid his hand horizontally through the air like a deejay.

"No." Erica shook her head. "I'm not angry with you."

"Cool."

"So, you like these meetings or whatever?" Erica asked cautiously.

Ted shrugged. "Some of them are okay."

"But they work, sort of, right? 'Cause you're not drinking."

"I guess," Ted agreed. "It's just a lot of people talking about random stuff."

Erica's cell phone rattled against her desk like a wooden snare drum. She flipped open the display panel. L CELL scrolled across the screen.

Ted looked down at his Casio. "I should probably start walking to my meeting."

Erica's thumb curled around the plastic faceplate and landed on SEND. "Hey," she said into the receiver. "Hold on a sec."

Ted waved apologetically and nodded toward the door. "I'll see you later," he mouthed.

"Ted." Erica dropped the cell phone to her shoulder. "Thanks for telling me."

Ted grasped the doorknob and felt the metal sphere frost his palm. "No problem."

"And don't worry," Erica whispered. "I'm good at keeping secrets."

Ted smiled. "I know."

Date: Saturday, 20 Sep 15:11:35
From: MichaelFIN@Highsmith.com
To: TedFIN@Highsmith.com

Cheers,

I feel truly dreadful about your recent communiqué. I trust you absolutely, my friend, and I promise that my compulsive information gathering is entirely electronic in nature. Armed with E's social security number and various passwords, I'm frequently overtaken by the need to monitor her bank statements and credit card activities. Rest assured, however, I am not sifting through university mailboxes or snooping around street corners!

You must understand that my harmless digging is a personality quirk that often takes on a life of its own. My psychoanalyst, a Burmese expatriate and a strict Freudian, attributes this neurosis to my parents' untimely departure, and I pray you will learn to forgive my obsessive tendencies. You are my partner, first and foremost, and I should be lost without you.

Caringly,
Michael

Date: Sunday, 21 Sep 11:40:43
From: TedFIN@Highsmith.com
To: MichaelFIN@Highsmith.com

Okay. I don't really have much to write. I haven't seen E. around for the last couple days because I think she's studying a lot. She's signed up for a bunch of music classes but you probably already know all about that.
T.

ep149846: no . . . i talked with his roommate ted and he said the asshole didn't remember a thing

DrMTRudas: And this is good news, I assume?

***DrMTRudas castles

ep149846: yes . . . very very good news . . . quit playing defensively doc

DrMTRudas: Then I'm happy for you.

ep149846: ted is actually a really amazing guy . . . we talked for a bit and he told me a bunch of other stuff about himself and his life

DrMTRudas: What type of stuff?

ep149846: promised to secrecy

DrMTRudas: I see. That's nice that he trusts you so much.

***check

ep149846: yeah . . . he's one of the only real people i've met here

DrMTRudas: What do you mean by real?

ep149846: i don't know doc . . . real

DrMTRudas: Pretend I'm from another planet.

ep149846: i do

DrMTRudas: Then how would you describe 'real' Ted to me?

ep149846: i don't know . . . i guess i feel like i can be my alone self with him

DrMTRudas: I think that's a contradiction in terms, Erica.

ep149846: you know how you can't really feel like you know yourself unless you're alone . . . cause there're a million eyes on you or people telling you what to do or say or think . . . cause people are like static for the soul

DrMTRudas: I'm following you.

ep149846: well with a real person i can be myself around them . . . . my alone self

DrMTRudas: Interesting. That's the way many of my patients have described feelings of love and affection.

ep149846: fuck you

DrMTRudas: What? Sorry. It was just an observation.

ep149846: FUCK YOU

DrMTRudas: Easy on the caps.

ep149846: very funny . . . it wasn't a sexual thing

DrMTRudas: My comment was just a silly aside.

ep149846: aren't we supposed to be talking about MY SHIT

DrMTRudas: Okay. Did you pick up that book I suggested?

ep149846: yeah . . . no offense but it's a joke

DrMTRudas: Really? Why?

ep149846: when i see 'demeaning images' of woman on tv i'm supposed to 'verbally denounce' them

DrMTRudas: It's considered a very helpful book.

ep149846: when i see a skinny photo of a woman in a magazine i'm supposed to rip it out and shred it to pieces

DrMTRudas: Not every suggestion applies to you, Erica.

ep149846: oh you're right doctor r . . . that last one was from the chapter on bulimic hamsters

DrMTRudas: I know you're joking, but a few days ago, you admitted to breaking your own policy of abstinence

ep149846: are you planning an intervention yet . . . it might happen again

DrMTRudas: I'm simply a concerned therapist. I cannot fix you or control you. The best I can offer is a sympathetic ear and an open dialogue.

ep149846: no offense doc but you're making yourself sound pretty useless

DrMTRudas: If you decide you're interested in getting well, I can be of inestimable value.

ep149846: if not

DrMTRudas: If you decide to continue with an unsustainable pattern of self-destructive behavior, I will prove to be one of many innocent bystanders. As they say, the choice is yours.

ep149846: so you wont freak if I tell you it happened again

DrMTRudas: No. I can't stop a smoker from smoking, an alcoholic from drinking, a bulimic from bingeing. I can only ask if you're interested in stopping.

ep149846: well . . . i'm not sure of anything right now

DrMTRudas: Thank you for being honest with me.

ep149846: no prob

Date: Tuesday, 23 Sep 09:41:08
From: MichaelFIN@Highsmith.com
To: TedFIN@Highsmith.com

Cheers,

Given the current scarcity of human intelligence, C and I were hoping that you might find the time to have a coffee or a cocktail with E's roommate, M. Obviously, we would never encourage you to utter a suspicious breath but, if there were a casual opportunity to join M at your local Starbucks, we think she might be able to offer a unique perspective on E's welfare. Would this be possible? I certainly hope so.

Eagerly,
Michael

Date: Tuesday, 23 Sep 20:29:56
From: TedFIN@Highsmith.com
To: MichaelFIN@Highsmith.com

I'll see what I can do. I never agreed to do stuff like this so I don't really think it's fair to ask me. But I'll try if there's an easy opportunity.

T.

Date: Wednesday, 24 Sep 16:08:24
From: TedFIN@Highsmith.com
To: MichaelFIN@Highsmith.com

I stopped by M.'s table at the library this afternoon and said hi. We probably talked for ten minutes but E.'s name only came up a couple times. Here are the things: 1) E. listens to her iPod late at night and that annoys M. 2) E. can touch type really quickly. 3) E. should go out more on weekends. Sorry if this is kind of boring stuff but I don't think M. spends a lot of time in their room. She's got class and practice every day and I know how busy that can keep somebody.

T.

Erica stepped into the second-floor lounge, flicked off the light switch, and smiled at her flittering pulse. Gently sealing the door behind her, she tiptoed through a shadowland of polyester furniture and stray textbooks. She double-checked her watch: 4:13 A.M.

Erica swung her knapsack off her shoulder and sat down at the rubberized dinner table along the far wall. Softly tugging the knapsack's zipper along the seam, she paused at the track's vertex. She'd heard a noise—a toilet flush or cranky vending machine. She wasn't sure. She closed her eyes and listened for the soft *clop* of carpeted footsteps. All she could hear was the wind scratching against the double panes.

Erica flattened her palms against the tabletop and swept the surface with a lazy breaststroke. She could feel bread crumbs and shredded eraser sticking to her skin, and she clapped her hands together over the carpet. Reaching into her knapsack, she pulled out a cardboard box of Coffee Depot muffins. The green-and-yellow-striped box was decorated with wavy stencils of steaming coffee cups, and she ran her fingers delicately across the italicized slogan: *Fresh*.

The first time Erica walked into the Coffee Depot she wasn't looking to build a binge. A chain-smoking Italian girl from her music class had invited her and two other girls from her evening section, and she'd simply agreed. And standing in line, trying to decide between an iced latte and an iced mocha, she'd been forced to watch the rakish jock in front of her as he bought up the entire rack of chocolate-chip muffins. When the cashier had finally rung him up, the jointed blue screen had read *$3.00*. Erica's eyes had darted around the counter, searching for an explanation, and had eventually settled on the dry-erase board above the espresso jets— STUDY GROUP SPECIAL AFTER 7:00 P.M. By the time she'd ordered her iced latte, she'd already spotted the store hours and the MADE FRESH DAILY sign hanging next to the ice dispenser.

Opening the cardboard box, Erica unpacked the towering blueberry muffins and carefully filed them in a line, like a bed of nursery evergreens. She knew it wasn't the money that had seduced her. It was the acceptability. She'd used bakeries and donut shops before, but she'd never felt brave enough to go back to the same ones. Last year, the young woman who worked the late shift at Eli's Bread had remembered her face and had snottily asked, "Who's the party for *this* week?" Since then, she'd stuck to convenience stores and supermarkets and the anonymity of the infrared price scanner.

Erica rearranged the dozen muffins into the circle of a clock face, with the largest at the noon hour, and wiped her fingertips against her bathrobe. She loved being able to calculate the calories and ingredients beforehand, but tonight she felt a panicky thrill at each muffin's homemade secrecy. She'd guessed three hundred and fifty calories per, but staring at twelve and seven o'clock, she decided to average it out at three hundred and seventy-five. Fat was easier: twelve grams, maybe fifteen, judging from the oily residue.

She lifted her iPod from the side pocket of the knapsack and balanced the earbuds so that their miniature speakers were pointing directly at her. Erica had been planning on Janis Joplin all evening. She debated plugging in one of the earbuds, but without a dead bolt she needed to be able to hear the hallway.

As she slipped her hand into her bathrobe's front pocket, Erica's fingertips tickled the grooved circumferences of her three quarters. She'd inspected every bathroom in the building, and the best candidate was the first-floor handicapped bathroom next to the laundry machines. She'd measured it at fourteen paces from the nearest dorm room. With an empty dryer grinding away, she knew she'd be safe.

Erica unpacked her twelve-ounce bottle of Poland Spring and meticulously reviewed her mental checklist. The only thing that still worried her was the walk. She'd hit four thousand calories dozens of times, but she'd never had to take more than a few steps afterward. A flight of stairs could be tricky, especially with the sugar spike.

Erica punched Janis's "Move Over" into her iPod and waited for her pulse to meet the backbeat of the bass drum. She wasn't sure how long she'd need, but she promised herself that she'd only play the song three times, even if she was stuck at eight or nine o'clock. Three times at three minutes forty-three seconds was a little over eleven minutes, and eleven plus a walk was going to be a stretch.

Erica placed her palm firmly over the cone of the one o'clock muffin and split the cake in two. Stretching her jaw, she slid the base onto her tongue. Saliva gripped the ridged walls of the muffin, and she pressed the bite against the roof of her mouth. Her jaw squeezed the air out of the dough. Blueberries and canola oil swamped her sinuses as her spit raced to soften the sweet sponge. Erica felt her throat twist, then capture a pair of lumps.

Collapsing the top of the muffin, she wedged the folded disc into her right cheek and squashed it against her molars. Erica drummed her thumbs against the edge of the table and hummed, *You say that it's over, baby.* Then she lifted the two o'clock muffin and swished a drink of water. She smiled with relief as a sugared chill swept through her stomach.

Hinges hissed, and the door to the lounge swung open. A cool gust slapped Erica's chest. Her shoulders clenched; she dropped the muffin. It wobbled along the tabletop and then exploded against the carpet.

Through the frame of the alcove kitchen pass-through, Erica saw the glint of a shoulder muscle. The back of a torso glided past the electric stove coils. An arm slapped the sink nozzle. Water splashed into the metal basin, and she suddenly recognized the white elastic of Ted's warm-up pants.

The soggy dough nestled in Erica's stomach pressed against her bladder, and she sat forward and softly yanked the earbuds from her iPod. She begged her hands to gather the muffins, to throw them back into her knapsack, but she was too afraid to move. Ted raised his water bottle to the tap and muted the rush of the faucet. Erica couldn't decide if he was sleepwalking or just oblivious. It had taken her eyes a few minutes to adjust to the light, and she sat there silently praying.

Staring down at her broken circle, Erica realized her fingernails were digging into the edge of the table. She'd been interrupted before—a Sikh limo driver with a package for her father, the Portuguese woman in 3B who'd borrowed a whisk from their housekeeper—but she'd never been walked in on. Pinching her lower lip with her canines, she promised a deal: *Let me escape, and I'll stop.*

Ted lifted the water bottle, tilted his neck back, and sucked on a cloudy red liquid. The snap of broken suction filled the lounge, and Erica listened to the soft gasp of his lungs. Ted rested his palms on the Formica countertop like he was preparing to lift himself into a push-up. Then his face twisted to the side. Erica felt a pellet of sweat sticking to her cheek. Her vision suddenly blurred. Images, shapes quivered.

Ted spun around on the ball of his foot and stared through the pass-through at Erica's crestfallen pose. From his height, he could trace the pale river of her scalp.

"Hey," Ted said, yawning.

"Hello," Erica muttered, hating the brittle sound of her voice.

"You scared me."

"You scared me, too," she whispered.

Ted studied her wilted shoulders, trying to decide if she was upset or frightened. "I guess we're both pretty terrible sleepers."

Erica surveyed the tabletop and then nodded faintly. She could tell he hadn't noticed the ring of muffins yet, and she imagined herself lifting one in the air like a shortstop and hurling it at his nervous grin.

"I still drink Gatorade. Powdered," Ted said, stepping out of the kitchen alcove and into the center of the lounge. "I don't know why the stuff relaxes me, but it does."

Dropping her glance, Erica followed Ted's bare feet across the carpeting. She could read in the slight hesitation of his step the moment he spotted her Coffee Depot spread, and her mind sped through useless excuses: *They were here when I sat down; I was leaving them out for people; I just baked them in the first-floor kitchen.* Erica's pleas ricocheted, and she was immediately disgusted with herself, with her excuses, with Ted. She looked up at him, expecting to see a sickened smirk. Ted was staring straight down at the floor, anxiously jiggling his water bottle.

"What?" Erica said. Her chest was trembling like she was about to sneeze.

Tracing his fingers along his collarbone, Ted felt the stale layer of sweat stuck to his skin. He was instantly terrified of talking, not talking, waiting to talk. "Nothing."

"Say it!" she declared angrily.

"What?" he asked without raising his eyes. He could feel how embarrassed she was, and he just wanted to run.

"You're fucking useless."

Ted lifted his chin. "I think I'm going to go back to my room."

"Fucking coward."

"I haven't done anything."

"Exactly," Erica said cruelly. "You're just fucking judging me." Making a fist in the air, she dropped her gavel on top of the nine o'clock muffin and drove it into the tabletop.

"You're wrong."

"Am I?"

"There's a difference. I mean there's a difference between—"

Erica turned back to the table and shook her head dismissively. "Get out of my face."

"I don't give a shit what you do," Ted said, exasperated. "It's pretty much your own fucking business, okay?"

Erica laughed. "Is that what they teach you at your Holy Roller meetings?"

"Fuck you." Ted started for the door.

"You fucking suck."

Ted twisted the doorknob and paused, just inside the doorway. "Deal with your own shit."

"I am!" she shouted as Ted slammed the door behind him.

Erica sprang up from the table and snatched her knapsack off the floor. Spreading the flaps of the bag, she tossed the flattened muffin into the empty canvas and then proceeded to sidearm the rest of the circle into her knapsack, one by one, each one harder than the last. She searched the table for the cap to her Poland Spring and gave up and threw the topless bottle into the mix. The rhythmic exchange of air and water flooded the leather base of the bag.

Squatting down on one knee, Erica gathered the fractured pieces of her final muffin off the carpet. She brushed the crumbs into the knapsack, wiped her hands against her bathrobe, and then collected the quarters in her pocket. The coins splayed across her palm, and she slung the stack into the knapsack like she was skipping a handful of stones. Zipping the bag shut, she dropped it to the floor and sat back down at the table.

Erica pinched the top of her thigh in between her fingernails, waiting for the dull throbbing in her gut to metastasize. Her mind kept replaying Ted's last words in a sluggish echo, and she found herself rehearsing different replies: *What the fuck do you know! Go fuck yourself! Get out of my face, you loser!* Closing her eyes, Erica filled her lungs with two rushed breaths. "Wrong," she whispered. "Wrong. Wrong. Wrong."

Erica slipped the iPod into the front pocket of her bathrobe and lifted the knapsack by its padded straps. Walking into the kitchen, she snapped open the lid on the plastic garbage can and tossed the bag inside. The knapsack settled on top of a stack of grocery bags, and Erica watched as Poland Spring gathered in the paper creases. Then she reached into the garbage can, slid her hand underneath the grocery bags, and flipped them over so that her knapsack fell to the bottom of the pail.

As she stepped back into the hallway, Erica's joints felt so fragile she worried she wasn't going to make it all the way to her room. If she tripped, she was convinced she'd splinter into a pile of muscle and cracked bone.

Frosted prickles stung the balls of her feet, and her arches sank into the hallway carpet. Searching the floor, Erica stared down at the pools of red liquid that sprang up between her toes and drained off her nails. Her first thought was blood. Then Erica realized she was standing in the center of an enormous puddle, a spill, and she looked over both her shoulders, trying to gauge its circumference. The splatter seemed to have started several feet behind her. A thin stream ran parallel to the tile wall and then splashed into a bell shape, like the shadow of a tulip.

Ted. Erica smiled, embarrassed that she'd been frightened by Ted's Gatorade. She pictured him walking arrogantly back down the hallway, muttering the word *bitch*, but she'd gotten to him. There was no question about it. Squishing her slick toes together, she decided it was the night's lone victory.

Erica stepped through Ted's puddle and dragged her feet dry along the carpeting. She checked her watch again: 4:31 A.M. She had music theory in five hours, and she knew she wasn't going to be able to fall asleep. She wouldn't have minded just lying in bed and listening to her iPod, but Maisy's rattle peaked around sunrise.

Erica twirled her doorknob and pressed her big toe against the corner of the door. A parallelogram of hallway light stretched across her striped throw rug. Walking softly over to her desk, she lifted the desk drawer, guided it silently open, and set it back down. She grabbed her Citibank box of checks and slid the stiff top off. Her two Rite Aid pill bottles were lying snugly next to each other, their pastel warning stickers rocking gently in their cradle. Erica picked up the wide orange canister and jostled the Prozac tablets—lime jelly beans leveled off in the middle of the cylinder. She hadn't popped the top in nearly a week.

Erica tossed the Prozac bottle into her trash can and turned to check on her roommate. Maisy was yawning into her starry pillow, and Erica eyed her contorted forearms, wondering what might be stirring in a dreamscape Needham, Massachusetts. Then Erica grabbed the other pill bottle and pressed firmly on the disc top. Snapping it open, she poured out a handful of ten-milligram Ambien tablets. The white pills reminded her of Fun-Dip sugar sticks, and she chose two broken halves.

Dropping the pair of halves onto her tongue, Erica crushed them between her molars. Tart sludge spilled down into her gums and numbed her lips. A nauseous shiver tickled her throat. Swirling her tongue through the bitter chalk, Erica reminded herself that she was saving sleep wait time. A chewed Ambien was fifteen minutes away; a swallowed might be twenty or twenty-five. She took a swig from a flat can of Fresca and swished it around.

Stepping over to her bed, Erica yanked the quilt aside and tossed her bathrobe onto the arm of her desk chair. She lay down on the icy sheets, squeezed her eyes closed, and started her countdown at one thousand. Four floodlit digits flashed across the back of her eyelids.

Date: Thursday, 25 Sep 08:47:34
From: MichaelFIN@Highsmith.com
To: TedFIN@Highsmith.com

Cheers,

Alas, E's roommate has proven to be as useless as I once feared. What did we expect from a girl whose college essay focused on multi-state penny drives? Regardless, thank you for trying. I hope it wasn't too, too awkward.

More importantly, I'm afraid we've hit a bit of a snag. E's Blue Cross prescription records fail to reflect her monthly Prozac refill. While there are a number of plausible explanations, ranging from a cash payment to a supply of samples, I naturally assume the worst and am preparing to notify C.

Since you seem to be quite familiar with E's schedule, I hoped that you might be able to check the date on her pill bottle (N.B. You'll be looking for a bottle of green-and-white 20mg Prozac pills). I realize this is slightly invasive, but it is far better than involving her psychiatrist, or worse yet, her overbearing father. As I mentioned in a previous note, it is our primary responsibility to protect E in her fragile state, and this is your first bona fide opportunity to prove your unquestionable utility.

Lastly, as an aside, I was reviewing E's Hotmail emails from this past week, and I thought you would enjoy reading her kind description of you. I've clipped the relevant passage.
>
>DATE: Wed, 17 Sep 10:16:22
>From: XXXXX@Hotmail.com
>To: XXXXXX@Lycos.com
>Cc:
>

>of course everybody's terrified. i mean you see these groups of like ten or twenty frosh marching to the cafeteria every night to burn their meal credits together. it feels like some sort of psych experiment in social anxiety or group dynamics. whatever. i've met a few kids who aren't totally generic and i guess that'll do for now. there's an indian girl from san francisco who invited me to this amazing screening of 'it happened one night.' she's a jainist (sp???) and she was telling me all this unbelievable stuff about how she's not allowed in her family's kitchen when she's got her menses. how fucked up is that? i still like hanging out with that cute basketball player i told you about. i think my roommate has a crush on him but it's probably just because she knows we've hung out and he's only said five words to her. it's going to be a miracle if I don't smother her in the middle of the night with one of her embroidered pillows. — e

>

Nice work, young man. I found it quite reassuring, and of course, your efforts will not go unrewarded.

Appreciatively,
Michael

Date: Thursday, 25 Sep 15:32:54
From: TedFIN@Highsmith.com
To: MichaelFIN@Highsmith.com

You are like the fucking CIA. Are you tracking my fantasy football team? Because I'm open to suggestions or trade ideas. I'll look around her room as soon as I get a chance but I'm not emptying drawers or picking locks or anything as ridiculous as that. For all we know she carries the pills in her purse. And please don't forward me

any more of her emails. I have enough trouble falling asleep at night. Who knows if I'm even the guy she's talking about since I'm not a basketball player anymore?
T.

Date: Thursday, 25 Sep 17:08:11
From: MichaelFIN@Highsmith.com
To: TedFIN@Highsmith.com

You must learn to take a compliment, my son.

_____

ep149846: i feel like bashing someone's face in
DrMTRudas: I understand.
ep149846: i'm serious
DrMTRudas: I understand. How do you think he feels?
ep149846: i don't fucking care . . . he just better keep his mouth shut
DrMTRudas: I bet he feels pretty terrible as well.
ep149846: I DON'T CARE
DrMTRudas: I only mention it because you described him as a very decent young man and I would imagine he's just as uncomfortable with the situation as you are.
ep149846: that's not fucking possible
DrMTRudas: This is the same young man who confided in you earlier this week, yes?
ep149846: yup
DrMTRudas: Then I think you're overlooking a very important point.
ep149846: and what would that be

DrMTRudas: Well, this young man also depends on you for secrecy, right?

ep149846: you think i should blackmail him

DrMTRudas: No. I think, perhaps, you're underestimating him. Given the fact that he's demonstrated a high level of trustworthiness, it seems entirely reasonable to me that he would respect your privacy.

ep149846: i get your theory but that's all it is . . . . a theory

DrMTRudas: Well, when do you plan on talking with him about it?

ep149846: are you out of your fucking mind . . . what's there to talk about

DrMTRudas: The mature course of action would be to sit down with him and explain your position, your concerns and hopes.

ep149846: and what position is that genius

DrMTRudas: Erica, this could be a very meaningful opportunity for you to confront some of your feelings and fears.

ep149846: fuck off

DrMTRudas: Then think about it at least.

ep149846: there's nothing to say . . . he knows what i was doing . . . i know what i was doing . . . end of story

DrMTRudas: I think you're underestimating him and underestimating yourself.

ep149846: what the fuck could he say that would make any difference

DrMTRudas: He could say exactly what I'm going to type right now: That I understand why it happened, that I don't blame you, that I like you as a person and want to help you get well.

ep149846: and what if he says i'm a fat crazy bitch

DrMTRudas: I sincerely doubt he'll say anything like that.

ep149846: easy for you to say

DrMTRudas: When was the last time you gave somebody the benefit of the doubt?

ep149846: when i left the womb

Date: Saturday, 27 Sep 11:50:22
From: TedFIN@Highsmith.com
To: MichaelFIN@Highsmith.com

I think I found what you're talking about so you can call off the cavalry. In the top drawer of her dresser she's got a real big prescription bottle full of Prozac pills. She filled it at the place on M. street and the date is from last week. It doesn't say whether she paid cash or anything like that but I guess she must have.
T.

Date: Saturday, 27 Sep 13:28:45
From: MichaelFIN@Highsmith.com
To: TedFIN@Highsmith.com

Cheers,

I owe you a debt of thanks!

Gratefully,
Michael

Ted slapped his thumb against the TAB key on his laptop and watched the blinking foul line skip across the screen. Sitting forward in his chair, he typed out *John Maynard Keynes*. Then he scrolled back through the text and deleted *Maynard*. It felt remedial to begin with a person's full name, like a book report.

Three days before Ted left for school, his father had bought the Dell laptop from the Home Depot staff supervisor for two hundred dollars, and Ted had already dropped another fifty of Michael's cash having the Computer Center install an Ethernet card. The glossy japan keyboard had arrived missing the CAPS LOCK key; only the cylindrical nub remained, and Ted had caught himself casually lying to James about its absence.

James kicked open their door and waddled into the room, bear-hugging his laundry bag to his MOLSON T-shirt. *"Buenos días,"* he bellowed, dropping the bag onto his mattress. "You eat yet?" James reached underneath his bed, rolled out a pair of twenty-pound dumbbells, and pulled them into a curl.

"I've got to get this accounting summary done," Ted said.

The keyboard's pin-sized speakers lit up with the first line of Frank Sinatra's "For Once in My Life." Ted looked down at the bottom-right corner of the screen and spotted the sandy envelope icon. The laptop was booby-trapped with Sinatra. A finished download triggered the "My Way" chorus. A shutdown or restart sparked "Strangers in the Night." Ted hadn't figured out how to disable the sound bytes, and surprisingly, James seemed to enjoy them.

"The Chairman of the Board," James declared, pausing midcurl to check his form.

Ted dragged his fingertip across the touch pad and double-clicked the envelope icon. The INBOX filled the screen. He stared at the emboldened top row of text, scratching his cursor over the name **Prakers, Erica**. Tilting his head back, Ted checked that James was still occupied with his dumbbells. Then he dropped his thumb on the left-click button.

Date: Saturday, 27 Sep 18:01:22
From: Prakers, Erica
To: York, Ted

if you don't even want to read this i'll
understand. i just needed to apologize for the
other night. you startled me (if that's the
right word) and i said a bunch of stuff that i
wish i hadn't. obviously i'd rather not make a
big deal out of this (my privacy is very
important to me) but i wanted to let you know
that what i said wasn't fair. anyway sorry you
caught me at a bad moment. i'd like to keep
being your friend. e.p.

Bowing forward, Ted hugged the frame of his keyboard with
his forearms. He'd imagined a one-word e-mail, a single note on
which everything else balanced: *Spy.*

James's strained breathing broke Ted's daze, and he quickly
minimized Erica's e-mail. He wanted to talk to her. He needed
to. Ted thought about walking over to Erica's room, but he
didn't have the right to barge in on her again. Besides, he figured,
she could be writing from any computer on campus.

Ted closed Erica's e-mail and clicked COMPOSE. He'd nearly
hit REPLY, but he didn't want James peeking over his shoulder
and spotting Erica's note. Tabbing down to the text box, he typed
out *Dear Erica* and then immediately erased it. *Dear* was too inti-
mate, but he couldn't begin with a casual *Hey* or *Hi.* Double-
clicking Erica's e-mail again, he realized she'd skipped right over
an opening. She'd just started. Ted minimized Erica's note,
punched the CAPS LOCK nub, and wrote the only sentence he was

sure of: *THANK YOU*. He hit the space bar and nodded to himself. It felt like the right way to begin.

Floating his fingers above the touch pad, Ted rehearsed his next few words and then stabbed at the keyboard. *I'D LIKE TO TALK WITH YOU WHEN YOU HAVE A SECOND*. The words felt formal, almost parental. Pressing down on BACKSPACE, he recaptured half the sentence. *WHEN YOU GET A SEC*. The cursor rested at the mouth of the *C,* and Ted quickly added *OR WHATEVER*.

Drumming his thumbs against his rib cage, Ted carefully reread the note. The all caps looked good, distinctive and secure, but he still needed an ending. He'd been impressed with Erica's elegant initials, and he wondered whether she'd also debated her signature. Ted knew he couldn't use any of his regulars—*Thanks, Peace, Sincerely*. It had to be friendly and respectful without seeming playful. His pinkie flicked the *T* and sped through *TRULY*. Then Ted dragged his cursor over the five letters, highlighting the text negative, and deleted it with a *B. BEST*. It wasn't the perfect word, but he meant it. He placed a comma at the base of the *T* and typed his first name.

Sliding the cursor up to SEND, Ted cocked his fingertip and squeezed his eyes shut. *Was Michael watching?* If he could hack into Erica's Hotmail account, he could probably slip through a college server. Ted quickly considered taping his reply to Erica's door, but Michael would've already seen her e-mail.

He curled his toes against the carpeting and tapped the left-click rectangle. The e-mail dissolved into a single pixel. Swiveling around on his chair, Ted tried to ignore the nervous tingles that were stinging his chest. James had both dumbbells raised directly above his scalp, and Ted could see deodorant snowflakes sticking to strands of his armpit hair.

"Hey, how much can you bench?" James exhaled.

"I don't know," Ted said, hoping to distract himself. "Why?"

James's front teeth pinched his lip as he reached the end of his set. "Two hundred?"

"Two-fifty, two seventy-five," Ted corrected.

"I knew it." James gasped as he dropped the dumbbells to the floor. "I bet Nate you'd fucking own him."

Ted shrugged. "I don't think I know him."

"He's my buddy from stats. And he's going to owe me twenty bucks."

"How's that?" Ted asked hesitantly.

"'Cause I told him you'd take him to school." James untied his laundry bag and wiped his forehead on a fresh towel. "So whenever you're free, we're walking over to the house and making ourselves ten bucks each."

"I—I—"

"For Once in My Life" broke Ted's stutter, and he twisted back toward the laptop. His hips whipped around, swinging his right kneecap into the front leg of the desk. Numbing static washed away the feeling in Ted's leg as he squinted at his INBOX. **Prakers, Erica** popped into the top slot and knocked her first e-mail down a step. Double-clicking her name, Ted whispered, "Please, please, please."

```
Date: Saturday, 27 Sep 18:04:41
From: Prakers, Erica
To: York, Ted


cOmE oN oVeR
```

Ted smiled at her alternating casing and typed *oKaY*. He was glad she'd noticed his CAPS LOCK, but he suddenly worried it seemed bossy.

"Ground control to Major Ted," James sang.

"Sorry," Ted said, hitting SEND. "We'll do it later."

"Nice."

Ted stood up from his chair and tried to shake the feeling back into his knee. He'd wanted a few hours to prepare for their conversation, but he could feel a swell of adrenaline escorting him toward the door.

Ted rapped his knuckles against Erica's doorknob and then gently turned the latch. Stepping through the doorway, he heard the clasp of Erica's laptop springing closed.

She was sitting at the foot of her bed in corduroys and a V-neck long-sleeve, and her laptop was balanced on her tightly crossed legs. "This time," Erica began, "I was expecting you."

"That's probably a good thing," Ted said, grinning uneasily. "Is Maisy coming back soon?"

"God, I hope not."

"I guess you guys aren't getting along too well." Ted lifted himself onto Maisy's mattress and peered out the window.

"It's like living with Little Orphan Annie."

Ted laughed, unsure exactly what she meant. "She's got the red hair."

"Have you ever tried to talk to her?"

"Just that time with you," he said proudly.

"Yeah." Erica slid the laptop onto her bed. "So you wanted to chat?" she asked, trying to gauge his mood.

Ted's fingers instinctively pinched Maisy's quilt. "Yeah." He needed to tell Erica that he understood bad moments, that he wanted to help her. "Well, I sort of thought we might."

"So quit stalling," she joked.

"Sorry. Just so you know, I haven't told anybody about anything. I mean, I wouldn't have even without you saying anything."

"Thank you," she whispered, searching his eyes and lips for tell-tale hesitation.

"I guess I just don't want you to think that I'm thinking lots of negative stuff about you, because I'm not. So—"

"I hadn't really thought about it."

"I should probably just tell you that I have a friend who does the same thing or whatever." Ted scratched at his sore right kneecap, tracing the shape of his sunken treasure. "I mean she's older than us, but she's talked about it a bunch in meetings—"

"That anonymous thing," Erica said, drawing quotation marks with her fingers.

"Yeah," Ted continued. "She actually went to some other program for it, I think."

Erica jerked her head toward the window and watched a gnat tap-dance along her window screen. Then she flipped open her laptop and hurriedly started typing. "What program?"

"Overeaters Anonymous," Ted said, trying to track her fingertip hopscotch. He knew Erica was describing how scatterbrained he was, and he cursed himself for not taking a few minutes to prepare.

Erica looked up from her laptop, wondering why she was suddenly feigning distraction. "Is that where you think I should go?"

"No," Ted said, stunned. "That's not what I—"

"I know."

"I mean you should do whatever you want."

"Well, thank you for giving me permission to be myself," Erica said bluntly.

"I—"

"I'm kidding," she interrupted. "Sort of."

Ted sat forward on Maisy's bed. "I should probably let you keep working or whatever."

"Wait," Erica said. "I have a pretty strange sense of humor sometimes."

"I guess."

"I mean you shouldn't take everything I say *so seriously*."

Ted tilted his chin and tried to soothe his stomach. "I kind of feel like you're the one taking my words too seriously."

"That's fair," Erica agreed, uncrossing her legs. "Listen. I know how fucked up it is. I mean, I've heard the Bingeing 101 lectures, and I've read the books, and I know, okay?"

Ted nodded.

"I just go through phases, and it's there, and then it always goes away."

"Do you want to stop or—I mean, do you like doing it?"

"Did you like drinking?"

"I loved it."

"Right," Erica said.

"But it kind of fucked up my life pretty badly," Ted added.

"And that's why you stopped?"

"Yeah."

Erica ran her palm along the corduroy grain of her calf. "And do you miss it?"

"Every day," Ted confessed. "Fuck, I missed it even when I *was* drinking."

"So how do you keep from going back?"

"I made a deal with my father. A promise," Ted explained. "I mean, he wouldn't have let me come to school otherwise."

Erica smiled. "You and I have a lot in common, Ted."

"I guess we do."

"So we've both got our thing, right?"

"Yeah."

"But you're not going to go around worrying about me, okay?"

"I'm not worried about you," Ted said, suddenly realizing it was the first time he'd deliberately lied to Erica. He searched for a retraction or qualification and then let go.

"You could've fooled me."

"I probably spend too much time listening to people struggling with stuff, like in the A program," he said, trying for a joke.

"And what do you say to them?" Erica asked curiously.

"Nothing." Ted shrugged. "I mean, people just talk or whatever. About drinking, life, anything that's going on really."

"That sounds like a nice thing, right?"

"It is, sort of."

Erica looked down at her flaked coat of nail polish and wondered if Ted had noticed her slight fingernails. "Yeah."

"Would you ever want to come with me? Like as my guest or whatever?"

"Where?"

"To a meeting."

Erica grinned. "Is that how you show a girl a good time?"

"No, I—" Ted scratched the streams of blush staining his cheeks. "I just meant that—"

"Why are you so nice to me?" Erica asked abruptly.

"I'm not trying to be," Ted insisted. "I mean, you know what I mean."

"I just know you kind of keep to yourself. Like you're not real talkative with anybody else, but you—"

"Probably 'cause most of the kids here aren't that interested in talking with me in the first place."

Erica hated watching somebody apologize for himself. "Why do you think that is?"

"I'm kind of from a different world than a lot of these people, like James."

"But I'm from the same world or whatever."

"Yeah," Ted began, letting his words gather. "But I guess you don't seem that happy about it."

Erica clapped her hands together and laughed. "You shouldn't be so quiet, Ted. You have some pretty interesting things going on up there."

Ted brushed his hand through his bangs. "I'm not *that* quiet. You just have to get to know me."

"You're a pretty mysterious guy," Erica teased.

"I'm not trying to be."

"Well, so, when do you go to *these meetings?*"

"I don't know," Ted said. "Pretty much every day, I guess."

"I meant what time of day?"

"Usually in the evening. If you're not busy with lots of stuff, you could come with me on Monday. The seven o'clock is an open meeting."

"What's today?"

"Saturday," he said.

"Monday at seven?"

Ted nodded. "Yeah."

"I've got section at eight-thirty, but all right," Erica agreed. "It's a date."

"Cool."

"Well, you know where to find me," Erica said, searching for a place to rest her hands. Habit had vanished, and she instantly felt as if she were wearing fluorescent oven mittens. Leaning toward her desk, she grabbed an empty can of Fresca.

"Cool." Ted pointed toward the door. "Well, I should—"

"Same."

He pushed himself back onto the carpet and started for the hallway.

"Ted," Erica began again.

"Yeah?" Ted said, spinning around.

"I know I can be a bitch sometimes. . . ." She paused. "But you're one of the only people at this school who I respect. So—"

"Me, too. I mean I feel the same way about you."

Erica lowered the soda can to her waist and nervously swiveled the flip top. "You can go now," she said, smiling to herself.

Date: Sunday, 28 Sep 08:11:56
From: MichaelFIN@Highsmith.com
To: TedFIN@Highsmith.com

Cheers,

While crafting my morning note, I answered a frantic phone call from one of my associates. He explained that you'd received an email from E's university account in which she apologized for an indeterminately vicious outburst. Having just read a faxed copy of her correspondence, I now find myself in a state of apoplectic shock. Needless to say, I demand that you immediately explicate not only the nature and substance of your disagreement, but also your foolhardy attempt at shielding it from me. If there still remains any ambiguity as to the seriousness of your indiscretion, let it end with this sentence: You cannot hide from the hidden.

Absolutely,
Michael

Date: Sunday, 28 Sep 13:46:22
From: TedFIN@Highsmith.com
To: MichaelFIN@Highsmith.com

I wasn't trying to HIDE anything from you. I guess I was just embarrassed or something. E. caught me leaving her room yesterday (I was looking for those pills) and I think she'd had a few drinks already in her. I told her I was looking for a highlighter (my backup plan) but she was a little tipsy and started yelling at me. I don't even remember what she said actually. Stuff about me being a freak but most of it was kind of garbled and drunk. I didn't really say much back to her and then she slammed the door to her room. That was it. So she apologized and I apologized and I think we both just want to pretend like it never happened. To be honest I thought you'd be furious at me for getting pinched. Sorry about everything. T.

Date: Sunday, 28 Sep 16:21:43
From: MichaelFIN@Highsmith.com
To: TedFIN@Highsmith.com

Cheers,

Forgive me my clichés, but when you've been in this business as long as I have, you learn that every player stumbles. The mark of a man is whether he knows how to right his unsteady stride, or whether he knows only the fall. Judging solely from your email, I am inclined to believe that you caught yourself rather artfully. Going forward, however, I must command you to err on the side of full disclosure. If you are ever uncertain about the relevance of a piece of information, you should always include it in your next correspondence. I am ready to forgive a mistake, not a habit.

Understandingly,
Michael

ep149846: he asked me out . . . sort of

DrMTRudas: How do you mean?

ep149846: to hang out monday night

DrMTRudas: I thought he would be nice, Erica, but not that nice. What are you guys going to do?

ep149846: can't say

DrMTRudas: I see. You must be very excited!

ep149846: i think i'm canceling

DrMTRudas: Well, it's nice to be asked nevertheless.

ep149846: whatever

DrMTRudas: How's the rest of your day going?

ep149846: fine . . . i haven't left my room

DrMTRudas: What about classes?

ep149846: skipped them

DrMTRudas: Are you still in bed?

ep149846: yup

DrMTRudas: Do you think you're anxious about hanging out with Ted?

ep149846: i think i'm anxious about having to be alive today

DrMTRudas: That bad. I'm sorry. My next appointment canceled so we can chat for as long as you like.

ep149846: thanks

DrMTRudas: Is there anything you do feel like doing?

ep149846: sleeping . . . listening to my music

DrMTRudas: How about a hot shower?

ep149846: i stopped the Prozac . . . just so you know

DrMTRudas: I guessed you might.

ep149846: are you angry with me

DrMTRudas: No, Erica. I don't think it was a wise decision, but I'm certainly not angry or upset with you.

ep149846: okay

DrMTRudas: When did you stop?

ep149846: two weeks ago or so . . . do you think i'm down from stopping the pills

DrMTRudas: To be honest, I'm more inclined to believe you've exhausted your body through poor nutrition.

ep149846: great

DrMTRudas: Can I ask you some blunt questions?

ep149846: go wild

DrMTRudas: No bullshit.

ep149846: you're cursing doc

DrMTRudas: No bullshit.

ep149846: fine

DrMTRudas: How many times a day are you bingeing/purging?

ep149846: 2-4 depending

DrMTRudas: How many full meals are you digesting each day?

ep149846: probably 1 . . . lunch in the cafeteria is usually safe

DrMTRudas: What does lunch consist of?

ep149846: salad . . . fruit and cottage cheese maybe

DrMTRudas: This can't continue, Erica. Your body can't take it.

ep149846: you don't know my body

DrMTRudas: I know the human body. I've spent my entire adult life studying it.

ep149846: and what in your infinite wisdom do you suggest i do

DrMTRudas: Would you be willing to try a new approach to recovery?

ep149846: i didn't even know i had an approach to recovery

DrMTRudas: Well, I think there are a variety of helpful options available to you.

ep149846: such as . . .

DrMTRudas: I'd suggest spending a week or two at a recovery center like Beginnings or Walker-Lukes. Rest up, eat well, re-hydrate yourself. Maybe talk with some people and learn some helpful recovery tools.

ep149846: i'm not going to a mental hospital

DrMTRudas: It's not even close to a mental hospital, Erica. Think of it as a health spa that you can leave anytime you want to.

ep149846: who works there

DrMTRudas: Doctors, nutritionists, physical fitness trainers, personal chefs, masseurs.

ep149846: and you can bolt whenever you want

DrMTRudas: Absolutely. You could check in and leave after an hour.

ep149846: who would know i was there

DrMTRudas: Not a soul.

ep149846: my father would

DrMTRudas: Not necessarily. If you had the means to pay out-of-pocket, there's no reason he'd have to know.

ep149846: you'd know

DrMTRudas: Again, not necessarily. I'd certainly like to know, but if you felt you wanted to be completely anonymous, I could provide you with a list of places and you could simply go.

ep149846: the people at the place would know who i was

DrMTRudas: Yes, they would know your name. However, believe me when I say that they are 100% confidential. Legally and professionally, they're bound by 100% confidentiality.

ep149846: how long have you been waiting to suggest this

DrMTRudas: A few weeks.

ep149846: why wait

DrMTRudas: This is the first time I've felt you'd even consider it.

ep149846: why do you think that is

DrMTRudas: Because you're exhausted. Because you're beginning to trust me.

ep149846: i think you're right doc

DrMTRudas: Thank you.

ep149846: i'm sorry

DrMTRudas: Again, I'm not upset with you, Erica. I think you're a marvelous young woman and my only hope is that I can help you help yourself.

ep149846: i'm still sorry

DrMTRudas: I understand.

ep149846: i'll think about it

DrMTRudas: Thank you.

———————————————————————

". . . so I'm stumbling down Laurel in the middle of the '98 snowstorm. I mean we got seven inches that night alone, and I'm trying to make it five blocks from The Clover Bar to my place on Brook . . ."

Ted leaned to his right and braced his hand on the metal frame of Erica's folding chair. "You want more coffee?" he asked, searching for something to say.

Erica had been completely still for the last twenty minutes, and Ted was convinced he'd made a mistake. Monday's Chapter Five meeting drew fifty or sixty people, and he should've started with a smaller, Big Book meeting.

". . . and I see this woman getting mugged on North Oak. She was probably two blocks ahead of me, but I take off in a flat sprint. . . ."

Erica shook her head stiffly and then picked Ted's *AA Meeting Booklet* off the gymnasium's waxed parquet. Delicately flipping through the pages, she watched the edges blossom into a wheat fan. She slid a ballpoint pen from her jeans and scribbled along the top of the booklet's PHONE NUMBERS page: *you sure it's cool for me to be here???*

". . . but I get to North Oak, and I square my shoulders like a lineman and just dive for the guy. I mean I was flat out . . ."

Reaching underneath his seat, Ted grabbed his accounting notebook and flipped it open. He lifted the pen from her fingers. *YES! I'm sure.*

". . . and, well, it turns out I'd tackled the cello case she was dragging. . . ."

The crowd erupted with applause, and a tight grin turned the corners of Erica's lips. She didn't know why she was smiling, but she felt like she didn't deserve to be.

". . . lying there covered in snow and cursing my head off, and this lady's just standing there terrified, trying to figure out why I'm spread-eagle on top of her cello . . ."

Erica stared down at the two chocolate-chip cookies resting on Ted's knee, wondering if he'd simply forgotten about them. She'd skipped dinner with a plastic tub of pineapple and honeydew, and she felt like curling up in her metal chair and taking a nap. *i feel like it's not okay or something,* she scripted, and offered the ballpoint back to Ted.

It's an open meeting so anyone is welcome.

". . . and I'm just starting to figure out what's going on and what kind of an idiot I am, and I say, 'I thought it was . . . I thought it was . . .'"

A group of bikers in the last row burst out in raucous clapping, and Ted measured the familiar acoustics of the gymnasium. On an indoor court, if you listened carefully enough to the crowd, Ted was convinced you could drive the paint blindfolded.

Erica inked the back flap of the meeting booklet. *but i don't believe what they/you believe etc. . . . .*

You don't have to believe anything. I promise that. Ted broke the top cookie in half and tucked it into his right cheek. Sipping his burned coffee, he suddenly understood why he'd broken his anonymity to Erica. It was crazy, but he knew he could only live with his one enormous lie if he destroyed every other secret between them.

Erica looped an uppercase *K*.

". . . Well, she was so impressed with my bravery that she wasn't even angry. I think she was more worried about me. . . ."

You having an okay time? Ted wrote, and playfully nudged her elbow.

Erica sat up, startled, and bumped him back. *yeah . . . definitely . . . i liked the last speaker a lot . . . the story about his wife getting sick was so so sad . . . i can't believe he just talks about it like that.*

". . . and the funny thing is that I'm twelve years in the rooms, and I still chuckle every time I see a big music case. . . ."

Erica laughed softly at the speaker's punch line. *so this is what you do all the time . . . listen to people tell crazy stories?*

Ted nodded and dipped his second cookie into his Styrofoam coffee cup.

does it work?

I guess. If you want it to.

but nobody's talking about how to stay sober???

Yeah. Ted scrunched his lips thoughtfully. *That's kind of true.*

". . . so thanks for letting me share, and thanks again to Terry for starting us off with such a solid qualification. . . ."

Ted shoved his hand inside his jeans pocket and slipped his finger between the flaps of his wallet. Peeling his Serenity Prayer card out of a side pocket, he handed the card to Erica and drew his finger underneath the first sentence of the AA Preamble: *Alcoholics Anonymous is a fellowship of men and women who share their experience, strength and hope with each other that they may solve their common problem and help others to recover from alcoholism.*

Erica flipped the Preamble over and started reading the Twelve Steps and the Twelve Traditions. Handing the card back to Ted, she twirled her pen like a baton. *god . . . god . . . god???*

The meeting's chairwoman rose to her feet. "Thanks, Bob. Name's Lucy, still an alcoholic."

"Lucy!" the group roared.

Ted shook his head definitively. *They say spiritual. Not christian or anything.*

but you have to believe in GOD.

". . . thanks to Terry for such a great lead, and welcome to the newcomers. Keep coming back. It works if you work it."

You're supposed to believe in something but that can be anything. Pretty much anything that isn't you.

do you believe in god then?

I believe in a basketball—Spalding game ball. Sports are stupid metaphors or whatever but it makes sense to me.

Erica grinned. *you don't mind i'm being kind of critical right? sorry if—*

Ted plucked the pen from Erica's grasp. *Not at all. It's what I like about you: no filter.*

". . . but my sponsor's been encouraging me to just talk about how angry I am at my boss. . . ."

i guess . . . Erica jotted, trying to decide if he was mocking her.

You're not afraid to say what you mean. Ted drew a line through half of his sentence. *Mean what you say—you know.*

i've never understood the point of sugarcoating something.

"... It sounds so silly saying it out loud here, but inside my head I'm bouncing off the walls. ..."

Erica Prakers doesn't sugarcoat.

you make it sound like i have a reputation.

Ted smiled and rested his hand on top of Erica's knee, gripping the denim arch of her thigh. She lifted her hand from the seat cushion, and Ted slid their fingers together into a fist and gently squeezed her palm. "Only with me you do," he whispered reassuringly.

Erica quickly unbraided their fingers.

"Sorry," Ted mouthed, flinching away from her.

"I—" She looked over at Ted's hunched neck and begged for the softest words she could find. "I should get to section."

Erica stepped silently into the aisle and followed the half-court line all the way to the gymnasium's padded double doors.

Date: Tuesday, 30 Sep 01:08:50
From: MichaelFIN@Highsmith.com
To: TedFIN@Highsmith.com

Having just reviewed E's American Express bill for the month ending September 28th, I am thoroughly convinced that she has returned to her destructive pattern of bingeing and purging. For the last two weeks, E has made daily purchases at your local Stop & Shop with an average total price in excess of thirty dollars. Given the fact that she is currently enrolled in the University's full meal plan, I am naturally forced to assume that her expenditures are being used to support her life-threatening routine. As expected, I have put in a call to C to discuss the matter.

I must also confess that I am deeply troubled by your failure to spot the reemergence of E's disorder. I realize the necessarily secretive nature of her activities but, to be blunt, you seem simply clueless.

Date: Tuesday, 30 Sep 11:23:56
From: TedFIN@Highsmith.com
To: MichaelFIN@Highsmith.com

Chill!!! I think I have an explanation for all the stuff you're talking about. For the last couple weeks E.'s been cooking dinner in the lounge/kitchen with a bunch of other girls from the dorm. One of them is this Spanish girl and I know they go out and buy all this stuff to make Spanish dishes. Maybe E.'s paying for the groceries? I know I should've told you about this before but give me a day or two to ask around about it. It would suck if you or C. did anything and then it just turned out to be the fact that E.'s made friends with these girls. To be honest E. seems really happy these days.
T.

Date: Tuesday, 30 Sep 15:42:09
From: MichaelFIN@Highsmith.com
To: TedFIN@Highsmith.com

You've got twenty-four hours, Theodore. I hope, for your sake, that you're correct.

 OCTOBER

Date: Wednesday, 1 Oct 08:18:50
From: CharlesFIN@Highsmith.com
To: MichaelFIN@Highsmith.com

M - The kid's broken. Last couple emails make no
sense. Either he's handling us or he's smoking
crack or he's a fucking moron. Been trading calls
with Rudas but haven't connected yet. Already told
Erica I want her coming down this Friday for my
angio. I'll have a look with my own two eyes.
Double check the Stop-Shop story. Stay on this.—C

Date: Wednesday, 1 Oct 11:50:27
From: MichaelFIN@Highsmith.com
To: CharlesFIN@Highsmith.com

Cheers,

I appreciate and share your concerns, and I will redouble my efforts. I hasten to remind you, however, that our boy's simplicity is part of his natural charm. Take comfort in the fact that Ted's cost of deception grossly outweighs any conceivable benefit. If you'll forgive the pun, he doesn't have a leg to stand on.

Helpfully,
Michael

P.S. My lawyer is ready to assist in the second transfer.

```
Date: Thursday, 2 Oct 09:37:56
From: CharlesFIN@Highsmith.com
To: MichaelFIN@Highsmith.com
```

```
M—Don't sweat the green. Waiting to see how my girl
looks, sounds, acts. Want to see what I'm buying.—C
```

Erica crouched forward and spit a dollop of tart saliva into the toilet. The maroon globule spiraled atop the bowl's current and then dipped beneath the surface. Massaging her neck, she listened to the bass drum of her pulse thumping against her ears. Her throat felt like she'd just gargled a handful of gravel.

The bathroom walls were checkerboards of blue and white tiles, and Erica's watery eyes traced the thin grout grids that fastened each tile in place. She blurred her vision and saw a windowpane swell into railroad tracks and then twist into a satellite shot of midtown Manhattan. A cross tucked into a plus sign folded into a doorway of tic-tac-toes.

Erica watched the images dart and curl and fade. Closing her eyes, she cycled back through the paperback pages of *Anna Karenina*. She'd finally finished the novel that morning in the Quiet Room of the music library, and there was something cheerfully hypnotic about being able to visually review the first lines of the eight parts, like she was decoding the calculus of Tolstoy's prose.

Erica dug her fingers inside the pockets of her pajama pants and emptied the crumpled Hostess wrappers onto the floor. Grabbing a handful of sticky packaging, she ripped the wax paper into confetti strips and tossed the strips absently into the toilet. She gathered the remaining wrappers into a ball, yanked the flush handle, and dropped them into the groaning whirlpool.

Gripping the toilet seat, Erica pulled herself upright. She stepped over to the sink and twisted the cold-water tap. Dipping her fingers underneath the faucet, she watched bronzed specks of apple pie spiral into the drain. Erica leaned over and stretched her tongue into the cool stream. She spit a mouthful of water back into the sink and waved her hands dry. Unscrewing her miniature bottle of Scope, she filled her cheeks with sweet mint and then checked her watch. 1:37 A.M.

Erica picked her cell phone off the wings of the sink and dropped the empty container of mouthwash into the trash can. Wedging her thumbnail in between the plastic lips of her phone, she popped the top and depressed SEND. L CELL pulsed on the screen like roadside neon, and she tried to decide if Laura's double ring was a true major third.

"Hey, babe," Erica said into Laura's voice-mail bank. "Just wanted to let you know that I'm going to be in the city on Friday. They're inflating a balloon in my dad's chest, and I'm supposed to hold The Ferret's hand. Sounds like a fucking blast, right? Whatever. So we should get lunch or something. All right, later." She slapped the phone closed and twisted the bathroom door's dead bolt.

Erica stepped into the hallway and listened to the static hum of the fluorescent panels. Tiptoeing to the end of the hall, she flexed her calves and lifted herself up to the clerestory window. On Brook Street, a pair of headlights topped the hillside and then sloped down the incline. As she fell back on her heels, her feet locked in fifth position.

Erica walked back to her room. Twisting the doorknob, she noticed a set of green initials on the corner of her door's dry-erase board. QE-JWDLP LOOKING FOR P-FWAST. Erica smiled at Ted's abbreviations and felt warm blush splash against her cheeks. She tried to figure out how long his message had been there. She'd come back from Stop & Shop a little after midnight, and she was almost positive she would have spotted it then. Running her fingertips through the fresh ink, she pictured Ted carefully drawing the hyphens in *ex-jock* and *post-feminist*.

A gentle current lifted Erica across the carpeting, through the stairwell, and to the foot of Ted's double. She tapped her knuckles against Ted's peephole as goose bumps freckled her forearms. Stepping away from the door frame, she suddenly realized James might answer. Erica had successfully avoided hanging out with James since that morning, and she couldn't believe she'd forgotten about Ted's roommate. Seconds passed, paired, grouped, and then fell away.

Carefully turning their doorknob, Erica inched the door open. A slice of hallway light cut across James's empty mattress and night table and stretched an open-faced paperback into the shadow of a gull. Across the room, Erica spotted Ted's thick toes atop the bedpost. His body was tightly robed in his quilt, and she watched his flickering nostrils inflate his rib cage. Slipping inside, Erica balanced the weight of the door against the spring lock.

She stepped toward Ted's bed, delicately shifting her weight from arch to arch. Ted's right calf was folded underneath his thigh, and as Erica passed the midpoint of his mattress, she noticed a lightning bolt of scar tissue creasing his kneecap. The milky rivulet spilled down the center of his knee, and Erica imagined a doctor's stainless-steel snip hitting damp bone. Jerking her eyes away, she tried not to stare at Ted's bare chest. His left nipple was decorated with a halo of chest hair, and she felt a spiking urge to wind her fingertips around and around the darkened oval.

"Was I snoring?" Ted mumbled, squinting at Erica like he was stuck in the middle of a wink.

"Hey." Erica smiled at the nickel of drool spotting Ted's pillowcase.

"What time is it?"

"It's one-thirty. I didn't mean to wake you. . . ."

Ted propped himself up on his elbow. "No, it's cool," he said, patting his mattress invitingly.

Erica sat down on the corner of the bed and felt his warm body under the quilt. "Can't sleep," she said, shrugging.

"That sucks." Ted yawned.

"I'm sorry I walked out early."

"It's okay." Arching his neck, Ted double-checked James's vacant mattress.

"Okay," Erica repeated. "I noticed the scar. On your knee."

"It won't bite," he said, grinning nervously. The elastic band of Erica's underwear peeked above the waist of her pajama pants, and Ted scolded his drifting gaze.

"It's pretty . . . impressive."

"I guess it's got its own look." Ted flexed his knee and slipped it out from the hem of the quilt. "From the outside, it feels like I'm a robot."

"Can I touch it?" Erica asked.

"Sure. But it doesn't really feel like a knee or whatever."

Leaning forward, Erica settled her fingers on the choppy muscles of Ted's lower thigh, and she delicately rubbed the embedded metal cap. "Crazy," she murmured.

Ted trailed Erica's curious gaze, trying to verify the cool impressions of her fingertips. Since his surgery, his mind had a habit of re-creating tactile sensations. His doctor had dubbed it "filling in the blanks," and Ted had spent hours tapping his numb scars with the eraser-nub of a number-two pencil.

"Made in Germany," Ted said.

Erica drew a rectangle around his hamstring. "You were diving for a ball or something?"

Ted debated the final two words in her question. He knew a plain nod would do. "Car wreck," he said, pausing in between syllables, like he was straining to read a billboard.

"That's a basketball play?"

"No. It's when you drive a truck into a tree."

"You—"

"Yeah." Ted knew it was insane, but part of him still wished that he'd crashed into another car, that they'd both swerved or skidded or flipped, that he wasn't solely accountable.

"Drunk?"

Ted nodded. He felt like burrowing into the chilled underside of his pillow and dissolving his senses.

Struggling through an uneven breath, Erica collared Ted's ankle with her thumb and forefinger. She felt as if she'd swallowed a charcoal briquette, and the expanding heat was blotching her chest and throat and cheeks. Erica's thoughts coupled and then untwined, and she suddenly realized she needed to kiss him.

"I don't know what to say," Erica whispered.

"Me, too."

"Do you believe everything happens for a reason? I mean, all the bad shit."

Ted shrugged. "Not really."

"Me neither."

"It'd be nice, though."

"I know," Erica said, measuring the distance between their chins. If she leaned toward Ted's mouth, she was terrified she'd fall short and end up pressing her lips to his collarbone. "So let's agree that it does."

Ted smiled. "Okay."

"'Cause if you hadn't crashed your truck, you probably wouldn't be lying here talking with me about everything, right?"

"You're probably right."

Playfully crossing her eyes, Erica slipped her tongue out of her mouth like a lizard. "And I think you're a pretty great friend to have."

"I think you're pretty amazing yourself."

"Thank you." Erica leaned forward and drew Ted's quilt to his Adam's apple.

"Are—?" he stuttered. "Are—?"

Erica rested her lips on top of Ted's question. As she rocked forward, their tongues tapped and buckled, and she wove their legs together. Ted's hands curved around her waist, warming her hipbones, as she spilled kisses down his chin.

Pulling away from their kiss, Ted traced her cheekbone with his finger. "You have a really small tongue," he said, grinning.

"Are you a tongue expert?"

"Sorry. That was stupid."

Erica flattened her ear against his pec like she was eavesdropping. "That was a lot of things," she said, "but it wasn't stupid."

Ted steered Erica's lips back to his. He stretched his palm across her lower back and held her against his chest. He reached up to the cup of her bra; Erica twisted away.

"Sorry," she whispered into his pillow.

Ted's eyes blinked open. "I didn't mean to—"

"No, it's not that," she said, shaking her head.

"But I should've—"

"I want you to touch me," Erica began, surprised by how honest the words sounded out loud. "Just not yet, though, okay?"

Ted placed a kiss on the tip of Erica's nose. "Okay."

"Okay," she echoed.

Erica rolled off of Ted's chest and spotted kisses on his shoulder. Ted zigzagged his fingers through her curls and kneaded the muscles in her neck.

"This is really nice," Erica said, drawing pothooks around his nipple with her thumb.

Ted squeezed her hip. "I think I might be lucid dreaming or whatever."

"If you were dreaming"—she pinched his wrist—"would you really be dreaming about me?"

"If I were dreaming," Ted said, twisting toward her, "I'd probably know the perfect way to tell you I think you're beautiful."

Erica cradled herself in the fold of his elbow and closed her eyes. "That's probably the nicest thing anyone's ever said to me."

"I wasn't—I mean—"

"I know."

Ted stared up at his posters and the wide-ruled shadows made by his blinds. "I can't believe we're lying here together," he said, giddily.

Erica laughed softly. "Really?"

"Yeah." Ted scratched at his brow. "I mean, yeah."

"I feel safe with you, Ted. I mean you know me, good and bad."

"Same," Ted said, massaging her shoulders. "I think you're the only person in this dorm I trust."

"I know." Erica tapped a gentle beat on his thigh. "Why do we stay, then?"

"To compete in today's competitive workforce—"

Erica jabbed his stomach. "I'm serious."

"Where would we go?"

"Anywhere," she said, kissing his hand. "Toss a dart into a map."

"It'd be kind of lonely, right?"

"I'm already lonely," Erica declared.

Ted slid the heels of his feet against the concrete wall. "You'd probably get sick of me."

"I think *I'd* get on *your* nerves first. With all my questions and tangents and—"

"Nah," Ted drawled. "You help me make sense."

Erica grinned. "You mean because I'm always chattering away or in the bigger sense or whatever?"

Ted smiled and dropped his lips onto her forehead. "Yes."

The ceiling vents breathed stale heat as Ted watched James's bobble-head dolls swaying jerkily next to his clock radio: 4:04 A.M. Rocking back in James's desk chair, Ted tugged at his sticky bangs. His chin drooped sleepily onto the bow of his collarbone.

Ted swiveled back to his bed. Erica lay placidly underneath his quilt. Her open palms rested against the edges of the mattress, waiting to catch the sky, and the curly strands of her hair fanned out evenly around his striped pillowcase.

Ted snapped the top sheet from a legal pad and let it fall to the blotter. Plucking a pen from James's change cup, he pinched the bridge of his nose. *Dear Erica, I wrote this out because I know I wouldn't be able to say what I need to say in person. I know I wouldn't make sense of any of it. I don't deserve you—* Ted scratched his pen back through the introduction. Folding the sheet crisply in half, he tore off the failed top half and tossed it into the wastepaper basket.

Ted pressed the shorn bottom half of the page to the blotter. *Erica, There are things about me which have nothing to do with you or how amazing you are. If you could just get inside my head right now and understand how much I hate myself for everything—* Ted bit the end of his pen cap and ripped off the sentence fragment. He bounced the strip of paper into the wastepaper basket and stared back down at the quarter page. *Erica, I can't ask you to forgive me. You don't deserve me or your father or Michael or fucking Maisy or—*

Ted noticed that his fingers were shaking, and he crumpled the piece of paper into a spitball. Reaching into the pocket of his warm-up pants, he slid out his cell phone and scrolled through the PHONEBOOK. He tapped SEND and watched Michael's number illuminate the display panel. The line rang once and then stuttered into voice mail.

"Hello, Theodore. I'm wildly disappointed to have missed you, but, alas, I've run off on another errand. If you'll be so kind as to leave the nature of your call, I will return it as soon as is humanly possible. And if you're wondering why you're able to enjoy such a personal greeting, it is because I have devoted this new phone exclusively to you. I hope you feel as special as I know you are. Ciao." *Beep.*

A muscle twitch joggled the joints in Ted's hand, and he squeezed the phone to his ear. "I quit," he whispered. "I'm ending this, okay? Enough. I can't take this, and—I'll find a way to pay you back for the semester, and that's it, okay?"

Stabbing END, Ted shrugged his shoulder over his cheekbone and smeared the teardrops perched on his eyelids. He ripped the battery strip off the phone and propped his left leg on the corner of James's desk. Gripping the three-pronged plug of the Christmas lights between his toes, he slid the plastic nub into the wall socket. The string of miniature bulbs haloed the half-empty bottles of James's minibar. Ted slipped his fingers through a handle of José Cuervo tequila and watched the golden water crash against the label. He spun the grooved bottle cap and dropped it onto the desk.

Clamping his thumb over the mouth of the bottle, Ted flipped the handle upside down and felt the warm liquor wet his thumbprint. He rested the bottle back on the shelf and waved his hand through the air. The eighty-proof dew cooled his thumb, and he drew his thumbnail across his upper lip. Inhaling the sharp breeze, he felt agave perfume sear through his sinuses.

Ted picked a dusty highball from the minibar and studied the mahogany glaze staining the bottom of the glass. He couldn't decide if it was evaporated whiskey or scotch, but he smirked at James's amateur tolerance. There was no excuse for giving up on your pour.

Ted reached for the fifth of Jack Daniel's, splashed a double into the highball, and gently swirled the contents. The auburn whirlpool sloshed around the rim of the glass and wreathed Christmas lights across the ceiling. Closing his eyes, Ted lifted the highball to his chin and listened to the whiskey lapping against the glass.

"Fuck it," he muttered.

Ted tilted his wrist and warmed his lips with the sour blend.

Snaking his tongue into the highball, he felt the alcohol singe his taste buds. He slid down in the chair and tossed the shot back. The whiskey scalded his throat, and a sudden streak of lightness seemed to electrify his fingers and toes and lips. Exhaling a hot breath, he patted his stomach and waited for the smoldering itch to melt his gut.

Ted gripped the square bottle, pulled a full swig, and opened his throat. The whiskey punched at his chest and glazed his eyes. He whipped his head back again and sucked the glass neck of the bottle until he'd flooded his cheeks. Gasping for breath, Ted coughed into his palm and twisted through a fiery shiver.

Erica batted her stiff eyelashes. Her mouth tasted like sleep. "You okay?" she asked, surprised by her rusted whine.

"Yeah."

"You want to come back to bed?" She yawned and rubbed Ted's pillowcase.

"In a sec."

Erica sat up, twirling the quilt around her body. "What are you doing?"

"Is that a trick question?" Ted said, placing his lips to the bottle and taking another swig.

"Ted, this isn't funny."

Ted mopped his hair back against his scalp. "Yeah. I agree."

"But I thought you weren't supposed to be—"

"You think so? I'm not really sure of that."

"Ted, put the bottle down and talk to me," Erica pleaded.

"Erica, Erica, Erica," Ted sang. "Where would I be without you?"

"What did *I* do?"

"You? Nothing," Ted slurred, shaking his head like a Raggedy Ann doll. "You're perfect."

"Then why—"

"Because I drink," Ted shouted. "That's what I do."

"Okay." Erica nodded and wrapped her arms around her chest. "I guess I just thought you didn't want to. I mean . . ."

"One day at a time," Ted announced, and tipped the bottle. "Yesterday, sober. Today, drunk."

Erica wilted back to the bed. "I don't know—I just didn't expect this."

"Well, it's better that you start finding these things out before you start caring about me."

"I already care about you, Ted."

"Erica." He sighed. "I'm not the right guy for you."

"What are you talking about?"

"I'm just not the right guy for you," Ted repeated softly.

"How do you know?"

"Because," Ted declared, balancing the Jack Daniel's on his metal kneecap. "Because I could never be part of your New York world, and you're sure as shit never going to want to be part of mine."

"You think I care about money?"

Bullets of sweat dampened Ted's brow as he swung the bottle back to his lips. "Because you're twenty million fucking times smarter than me and—"

"Ted," Erica interrupted, hugging her pillow against her stomach. "Why are you doing this?"

"What?"

"This!" Erica said.

"*This* is who I am."

"Ted, I know—"

"I'm a fucking spy," Ted cried, and curled away from Erica, planting his forehead against the blotter.

Erica shook her head in disbelief. "What are you talking about?"

"A spy," he mouthed.

"Ted—"

"Three months ago," he said down to the floor. "This guy showed up at my folks' place. It was over, okay? Over. The smashup, my knee, my scholarship. It was all fucking over."

"Because you couldn't play basketball?" Erica asked.

"Because I was useless. I was fucking useless to this school, and this guy, this guy was willing to pay. I didn't know what the fuck to think."

"Who the hell would—"

"I didn't know. I didn't know anything. I just wanted out."

"Ted, you're not making any sense."

"And here's this guy, and he seems for real," Ted panted, "and he's like 'I'll pay your way. I'll fucking pay your way if you'll just keep an eye out for this rich girl . . . this rich girl from New York.' And I—I don't know what I was thinking. I wasn't—"

"Ted," Erica started. "This isn't fucking funny. I don't know what you—"

"They paid me to spy on you," Ted said, swaying forward and resting his head between his fists like a boxer. "To watch you."

"Ted," Erica yelled. "Who the fuck would pay you to spy on me?"

"Your father," he whispered.

"What?"

"Your father."

Erica's chest swelled open, and she folded her arms defiantly. "Ted, you have no fucking clue what kind of a guy my father is. He's the farthest thing from anything you've ever seen. He runs fucking—"

"Peninsula Markets."

"Oh, my God," Erica gasped as gathering tremors paralyzed her hands.

"On the twenty-ninth floor."

"Oh, my fucking God. Oh, my—"

"In a corner office," Ted recited.

"Fuck, fuck, fuck."

"Staring at the Colgate sign."

Erica crouched forward and pressed her outstretched palm against the wall. "This isn't happening," she mumbled as icy currents overran her forearms, zigzagging across her breast. "This isn't happening. This can't be happening."

"Erica." Ted's voice broke. "I didn't tell them anything."

"Oh, God. Oh, God. I can't fucking—breathe."

"I didn't tell them a fucking thing," Ted declared. "Nothing that mattered, okay? Nothing. All they fucking cared about was food."

"Why is this happening? Why is this fucking happening to me?" Erica asked, begging her toes to unclench. "This isn't real."

"I'm so sorry, Erica. I'm so fucking sorry."

"You bastard," she shouted.

"I had to tell you," Ted begged, and dug his knuckles into his temples. "I couldn't—"

"I can't believe any of this is real," Erica cried frantically. She reached into the wrinkled crook of her inner elbow and pinched the skin. "Please don't make this real in ten seconds."

"I'm—"

"I need to get out of this. I need this not to be real. I need—"

"Forget me," Ted moaned. "I don't deserve to know you or anything or fucking anybody."

"This can't be real. I can't have this be real."

"If you never want to speak to me again, I'll understand, and—"

"Just get the hell away from me!" Erica screamed.

Pushing himself to his feet, Ted grabbed the Jack Daniel's bottle off the blotter and stepped toward his bed. "Erica—"

"Get the fuck out of my face, you fucking liar!"

Ted waved the bottle in front of his chest like a divining rod. "I never lied to you."

"All you are is fucking lies!"

Ted spun around on his heel and walked clumsily toward the hallway. Throwing open the door to his room, he punched the metal door frame. "I never fucking lied to you," he yelled down the hallway.

Erica gripped the quilt in a tight fist and drove her hand into Ted's mattress. "Fuck, fuck, fuck!" she shouted, pounding her knuckles into the cover sheet like a flailing piston.

Date: Friday, 3 Oct 04:18:50
From: MichaelFIN@Highsmith.com
To: CharlesFIN@Highsmith.com

Cheers,

I am afraid I just received a particularly troublesome voicemail from our boy. For reasons unclear and varied, he has offered to withdraw himself from our program effective immediately. As you might imagine, I am rather embarrassed by Ted's reckless actions and I am also acutely aware of how frustrating this must be for you. For that, I can only offer my humblest apologies.

While this late-night snafu presents a problem, I am exceedingly confident that our boy's tantrum is nothing more than the proverbial freshman funk. Perhaps his early academic failings have shied him from the university entirely? Regardless, I will telephone Ted first thing in the morning and I am convinced that a lengthy conversation will provide the appropriate opportunity to renew his commitment.

Apologetically,
Michael

Scrolling through her PHONEBOOK, Erica punched SEND and waited for the line to catch. A popping ring fought against the static. She swung open the door to her closet and yanked a carry-on suitcase to the floor. Unzipping the bag, she grabbed a handful of underwear and athletic socks.

"Hel-lo," Doctor Rudas answered. "Hello?"

"It's Erica."

"Erica?" Doctor Rudas asked.

"Did you know?"

"Excuse me?"

"Did you know?" she shouted.

"What's going on?" Maisy said, sitting up in bed. She was wearing a baggy, blue KINGSTON SPRING BREAK T-shirt.

Erica waved to Maisy with her free hand. "I need to know, okay?"

Maisy scratched at the point of her nose. "What time is it?" She yawned and turned toward the window.

"Hold on," Doctor Rudas said, coughing. "Let me just go to my office. . . ."

Erica turned back to Maisy and shrugged indifferently.

"What the hell's wrong with you?" Maisy whined, folding her pillow over her face like a sleeping mask.

"Excuse me?" Erica said.

"It's four in the morning," Maisy groaned.

Tossing a pair of sneakers into her suitcase, Erica held the phone against her cheekbone.

"Erica, sorry," Doctor Rudas began again. "My wife's a very light sleeper."

Maisy rolled onto her stomach and tugged her quilt over her head. "You're nuts."

Erica kicked her closet door closed and stepped into the hallway. "It's the only fucking thing I need to know. That—"

"Erica, I really don't have a clue what you're asking me, and—"

"You know," Erica said, walking in tight figure eights. She noticed she was dampening her voice and immediately scolded herself. She didn't owe anybody silence.

"I don't."

Erica smacked her hand against the wall and walked over to the stairwell. "You knew the entire time, you fucking coward—"

"Erica," Doctor Rudas interrupted. "I know it's four-thirty-three A.M. and I know you're furious about something, but I have no clue—"

"You have no clue," Erica mimicked as she climbed the stairs to the fifth-floor landing.

"None."

Gripping the fireproof banister, Erica stared at the crimson rooftop exit door and the electric wiring circumnavigating the door frame. "And why should I fucking believe you?"

"Well, I can't see the danger in telling me what I supposedly know already."

"That's cute."

"It's not cute. It's the truth."

Erica's fingers swam across the brushed metal of the exit-door release paddle, testing the pressurized weight, and then punched the door open. No alarm. No siren. As she stepped out onto the dorm's tarred rooftop, a fall breeze dissolved the specks of fresh sweat clinging to her lower back.

"Erica—"

"Why'd you have to pick Ted?" Erica asked as she walked to the edge of the roof. Chapel spires poked through the early-morning clouds like a sunken galleon. Below, the lobby windows angled outward at forty-five degrees and sheltered dry squares of gravel. "Why couldn't it be Maisy or—"

"Erica, the only thing I know about Ted is what you've told me. I—"

"That's such bullshit. You knew what the fuck he—"

"I didn't," Doctor Rudas exclaimed. "I don't."

"Why'd it have to be Ted?" Erica repeated.

"Erica, please tell me what's going on."

Along Brook Street, coverlets of fog were settling in the empty parking spaces. "They paid him to fucking spy on me."

"Oh, Jesus," Doctor Rudas said.

"My father bought him—"

"Erica—"

"My fucking father—"

"How can you be sure?" Doctor Rudas finished.

"Ted told me," Erica gasped as she sat down on the rough tar. "He fucking told me himself."

"Oh, Erica, I'm so sorry."

"Why Ted?"

"I didn't know," Doctor Rudas declared. "I swear to you, I didn't know."

"Why—"

"Erica, you're going to be okay. I know it doesn't feel that way right now, but you have to believe me."

Erica lay down on her back and felt the icy rooftop frost her shoulder blades.

"Believe that I believe," Doctor Rudas continued.

"I can't, doc," Erica cried.

"Believe that I believe."

"I can't stay here. I can't. . . ."

"I understand."

A tear raced down Erica's cheek. "What the hell am I going to do?"

"I'm so sorry, Erica."

"Where the fuck can I go?"

"We can figure something out, okay?"

"I can't live like this," Erica began. "I—I need to disappear. This place and these people. I'm going to fucking kill somebody, doc. . . . Doctor Rudas?"

"Sorry," Doctor Rudas said. "I was just thinking."

"I need this not to be happening," Erica begged.

"Do you have a car?"

Date: Friday, 3 Oct 07:51:22
From: CharlesFIN@Highsmith.com
To: MichaelFIN@Highsmith.com

M—FUCKING UNBELIEVABLE! You're lost in the weeds on this kid. I saw this coming down the pike weeks ago. Fix this now or find a new client. Don't care how you do it. Get the kid back on board and I'll have my chat with Erica this afternoon. Will make the call from there. NO FUCK UPS!—C

Understood.

"Bro."

Ted sleepily flexed his jaw and felt the whiskey's sticky residue warming his tonsils. A fist rapped against his hipbone.

"Bro." James laughed. "It's two."

Inches from his face, Ted squinted at a pair of pennies and a mangled pen cap. Twisting around, he brushed his chapped lips against the polyester seam of a pillow cushion.

"Buddy, the RAs want you up."

"James?" Ted groaned and squeezed his eyes shut. Simmering itches burrowed underneath his scalp like stingers.

"Bro, I got you coffee."

"Leave me the fuck alone."

"You passed out in the lounge."

Ted squirmed against the couch's backrest, praying for James to lower his voice. "Yeah?" he mumbled, suddenly wondering if he was hanging upside down.

Ted felt a hand slide underneath his chest and tug him upright. His eyes blinked open as he watched the carpeting pitch forward; the hand tipped him back against the pillow cushions.

"When you do it, bro," James declared, "you really do it." He offered Ted a Styrofoam cup.

Tossing back the grainy coffee, Ted slumped down and eyed the empty bottle of Jack Daniel's standing in the center of the coffee table. "I'm done with classes, James."

"You and me both," James agreed. "Now ten-hut."

Ted placed his hands firmly on the couch's armrest. Vibrating currents of pain seemed to be shooting up through the carpeting, numbing his right leg.

"You can sleep as much as you want," James added.

"Yeah." Ted trudged around the coffee table and into the hallway. Steadying his hand against the wall, Ted saw himself stumbling out of his dorm room, stabbing his fingers inside his ears as Erica's voice tore down from the sky.

"James, for real," Ted drawled as he hobbled past the line of door frames. "I'm dropping out."

"Sounds like a plan," James said, patting Ted's shoulder.

Ted turned into their room and grabbed his water bottle off his desk. Kissing the plastic straw, he filled his gut with lukewarm Gatorade. "You'll have a single." Ted burped and collapsed on his bed.

"Now, why would I want that?"

Ted twirled his quilt around his body. Outside the window, the hum of a lawnmower scratched the air like a distant alarm clock.

"You're going to rally," James said. "A little bit of lunch and you'll be set straight."

The chirp of their cordless phone broke Ted's daze, and he ducked underneath his quilt. Bathing himself in the claustrophobic heat, he suddenly inhaled the sweet dew of Erica's shampoo. Ted's eyes slid closed, and he pressed his lips to the perfumed pillowcase.

"Bro," James shouted.

Ted peered out from behind his sheets, trying to shield his eyes from the sunlight. "What?"

"I think it's a prof." James tossed the handset onto Ted's bed and then yanked his desk drawer off its runners, shuffling the contents. He punted his flip-flops end over end into the ceiling tiles and stomped back out into the hallway.

"Yeah," Ted said, lifting the phone to his ear.

"You fucking told her, didn't you?" Michael yelled.

"H-hello?" Ted stuttered groggily.

"Why'd she call her shrink at four in the morning, Theodore?"

"Michael?" Ted slapped his palm against the bed frame and pulled himself upright.

"Do you realize how much fucking money you've cost me?"

"Michael, what the fuck are you even talking about?"

"Oh, let's see. Where to begin?" Michael cooed. "The prescription, for starters."

"Listen—"

"The one she never filled," Michael finished. "The one—"

"Michael, she's doing fine, okay? I mean, I just saw her at the library, and she's doing great."

"Really?" Michael asked sarcastically. "Then why, in your infinite wisdom, do you suppose she just charged twenty dollars' worth of gas at a Mobil station an hour away from campus?"

"That's a mistake," Ted said confidently. "Trust me. I just saw her."

"*You're* a mistake, you piece of white trash."

"Fuck you!" Ted yelled.

"Pack your bags, Theodore, this charade—"

"Let me talk to her," Ted insisted. "I—"

"Honestly, Ted. You'll be lucky if you ever speak to her again."

Beep.

Swinging his legs to the floor, Ted walked lethargically over to James's bedside table and grabbed a half-empty can of Milwaukee's Best. He gargled a mouthful of stale beer and waited for the familiar buzz of the first sip. "Fuck you," he repeated, lying back down on his bed.

Ted heard a soft knock on his door, and he looked up at Maisy. She was holding a bag of ice to her thigh, and a paperback copy of Goethe's *Faust* was hanging out of the chest pocket of her gymnastics sweatshirt.

"Everything okay?" Maisy asked. "I heard . . ."

Ted nodded and poured the bottom of the beer down his throat.

"I didn't know you were pledging," Maisy said, grinning at Ted's sallow complexion.

"Where is she?" Ted asked, ignoring her smile.

Maisy shrugged. "I was just going to ask you the same question."

Ted squeezed the beer can into a fist, bending a metal hourglass, and finger-rolled it onto the floor. "What the fuck does that mean?"

"Ted," Maisy began defensively, "she's out of her mind."

"Just tell her I need to talk to her," Ted said, suddenly exhausted.

"Okeydokey," Maisy sang, spinning around on her heel and starting back to her room.

Leaning off the edge of his bed, Ted grabbed his cell phone and plugged the battery back onto the faceplate. He dialed Erica's number and begged for a choppy ring. The feed crackled and launched him straight into voice mail. "This is Erica, and this is your fifteen seconds. To leave a message . . ." He pressed the number 1.

"Hey, it's me. It's Ted," he whispered. He rested his pinkie against the END key and then swung the phone back to his lips. "Erica, I'm so sorry. I—I just need to talk you, okay?"

James stepped lazily back into the room and arched his eyebrows at Ted. "I'm fucked," James announced, falling into his desk chair.

Shielding his palm around the mouthpiece, Ted glared at James. "I'm in my room. Okay, bye."

James drew a puck of Skoal from the back pocket of his chinos. "They stole my Merc, Teddy."

"Who did?" Ted said in disbelief. He lifted his laptop off his desk and double-clicked the Explorer icon, then stumbled through his Highsmith username and password. Ted's INBOX read 1 NEW MESSAGE.

```
Date: Friday, 3 Oct 13:27:08
From: CharlesFIN@Highsmith.com
To: MichaelFIN@Highsmith.com,
TedFIN@Highsmith.com


M & T—What the fuck is going on??? Where's my
daughter? She was supposed to be at Lenox Hill
two hours ago. THIS IS UNACCEPTABLE. Somebody
better give me an update. If my cell craps out,
call me at the hospital. 212-555-7800. Don't
know my room num yet.—C
```

James scooped a finger of wet tobacco and tucked it behind his lower lip. "I don't fucking know. Thieves."

Ted minimized the Web browser and grabbed his jeans off the bedpost. Yanking open the top drawer of his dresser, he slid his arms through a wife-beater and wiped the sleep dust from his eyes. "You're sure?" he asked, frantically trying to remember Erica's class schedule. If she wasn't at her music section, she'd be on the second floor of the sciences library.

"Well, the car's gone. And so are the keys," James said, pointing at his overturned desk drawer.

"How could someone . . ." Ted's voice faded as his thoughts wove together. Erica had probably seen the keys on James's desk.

James walked over to Ted's bed and picked up the cordless phone. "I'm calling the cops."

"It's not stolen," Ted started, dizzy with adrenaline. He suddenly realized he needed a car. He needed to drive.

"Fuck it's not." James spit absently into the recycling bin and punched 911.

"I know who took it, James. I mean, I'm almost positive."

"What the fuck are you talking about?"

"I know," Ted repeated. "Hang it up."

James slammed the cordless phone back onto the cradle. "Who taxed my ride, Ted?"

"You have to promise me you won't call the cops. I mean, you have to give me a couple hours, okay?" Ted begged.

"Fuck you," James said. "Who jacked my wheels?"

Ted crossed his arms tightly. "Just a couple hours."

"Three."

"Erica Prakers."

James smacked the face of his desk. "That fucking bitch."

"It's not like that," Ted said, wiggling his hands.

"And why the fuck couldn't Princess buy her own damn Merc?"

"Something came up."

"But she's coming back with it? I mean, if it's even fucking her."

"Yeah," Ted agreed. "Don't worry about it, okay? She's not a thief."

James slipped his toes back into the webbings of his flip-flops. "Well, she can explain that to the state troopers."

"You promise you'll wait?"

"Hey, I'm a man of my word. I'm going to go smoke at the House, play a little Madden, a little Beirut. Five o'clock rolls around, no Merc, you know the rest."

"Thank you," Ted said, imagining James's escape into a case of

Milwaukee's Best. James wouldn't have to move all day.

"Hey," James laughed, pointing innocently at the center of his chest. "I'm a friendly guy." He reached out and gripped Ted's hand in a firm shake. "I hope you're right, buddy."

"Thanks."

James flashed two fingers over his shoulder. "Late." His rubber soles smacked down the marble steps, and the pressurized hinges of the front security door whistled up the stairwell.

Tugging his blue-green flannel off the metal hanger, Ted fastened every other button. He knelt down on the carpet, slid out the bottom drawer of his desk, and lifted his two reams of blank paper. He pinched Michael's manila envelope. There was still $440 left, and Ted rolled the twenties into a tight spiral. Burying the cash in the back pocket of his jeans, he found his Nikes and hurriedly twisted a pair of double knots.

Ted walked quickly down the hallway, rapping his knuckles against each of his neighbors' doors. Debbie's voice carried out into the corridor, and Ted reversed his stride.

Debbie was still lying underneath her comforter, surrounded by an audience of thick highlighters. Her *Introductory Neuroscience* textbook was propped on her stomach, and she'd clipped her bangs with a jade hair clip.

"What happened to you?" Debbie asked, bookmarking her page with her ID card.

"Nothing, really," Ted said, trying to slow his breathing. "I was just wondering if you had a car."

"Yeah. What's up?" she asked, concerned.

"Can I rent it for the day for a hundred bucks?"

Debbie sat up against her stack of pillows. "Are you okay?"

"Yeah, it's kind of a family emergency, I guess."

"You're going to drive to Illinois—"

"No," Ted interrupted, suddenly wondering if that was the best idea he'd heard all semester. "But I'm happy to pay for gas and use and whatever."

"Okay." Debbie studied Ted's nervous grimace and then pointed to her bookshelf. "The keys are on top of my DVDs. It's the blue Jetta out on Brook, by the mailbox."

"Thank you."

"But forget about the money," Debbie said, shaking her head. "I don't charge friends."

Ted plucked the car keys off her copy of *Roman Holiday*. "Thanks. I'll fill it up."

"No worries."

Ted nodded and then turned back to the hallway.

"Be safe, Ted."

"Thanks," he shouted as he reached the staircase.

Hopping down the stairs, Ted felt his kneecap jostling against bone, and he gripped the banister. He pushed open the door on Brook Street and spun Debbie's key chain around his finger. Counting backward, he realized it had been nearly five months since he'd driven a car.

Ted pinched the DOOR OPEN button on the Volkswagen key and listened to the locks pop. Opening the driver's-side door, he found the metal handlebar beneath the seat and slid the chair back on its track. Ted sat down on the slate-gray vinyl and tapped his right foot against the gas pedal, trying to remember how hard he needed to press the accelerator. He guessed the Jetta's engine was half the size of his four-liter truck, but he was ready for a pair of sharp brakes. Sliding the key into the ignition slot, he twisted through the soft resistance. The engine turned and sent a shiver through the steel frame.

Ted suddenly worried that his metal kneecap might numb the

feel of the asphalt. Crossing his legs, he used the arch of his left Nike to slide off his right sneaker. He curled his toes around the accelerator pedal and tested the cool rubber.

Flipping through his CALL LOG, Ted highlighted ERICA CELL and hit SEND. The popping static faded into a double ring. The jingle sounded again, and then the line disappeared into Erica's voice mail bank.

"Hey, it's me again. I think your phone is off or whatever. It's straight to voice mail so . . . so . . ." Ted stuttered, and rocked back into the headrest. "So just call me on my cell, okay? I'm coming to New York. I don't know why. I mean, I know why but . . . I just need to talk to you, okay?" Ted's chest was shivering against his T-shirt, and he suddenly felt like he was hyperventilating. "I—" He pressed END and skipped the phone angrily across the passenger seat.

Date: Friday, 3 Oct 15:50:09
From: MichaelFIN@Highsmith.com
To: CharlesFIN@Highsmith.com

Cheers,

The situation has developed since my last email. Ted and I had a brief conversation this afternoon and I think it is very unlikely that he'll resume his agreed-upon responsibilities. Naturally, I will ensure that he absents himself from the university within the next twenty-four hours.

While Ted's resignation is disappointing, he was able to provide conclusive proof that Erica has returned to her self-abusive pattern.

Apparently, Erica's roommate caught her in flagrante delicto and shared the information with our boy. Based on Ted's revelation and the overwhelming credit card evidence at our disposal, I am entirely convinced that Erica should also be withdrawn from school at your earliest convenience.

As for Erica's current whereabouts, I assumed she was already in the city. Perhaps, her flight or train was delayed.

Finally, given the abbreviated scope of my assignment, I will expect the final $225,000 by the close of business tomorrow. I'd love to tidy this up as soon as possible.

Sincerely,
Michael

Erica stepped around an orphaned traffic cone glazed with gravel dust and waited for the traffic signal. Across First Avenue, two mailmen stood behind a striped delivery truck, waving the driver in opposite directions. The truck's warning siren pulsed to the beat of the flashing crosswalk, and Erica tapped the two-four beat on her thigh.

Cutting across the intersection, Erica tugged the sleeves of her sweater over her fingers and inhaled the damp city breeze. She could still feel her mind revving, and she tried to remember when she'd finished her last Diet Coke. She'd spent the drive working through a six-pack, but the caffeinated fever was just beginning to break.

Erica passed the fluorescent oak-tag billboards of a liquor store and the Book Nook's display case of New York City travel guides.

Stopping underneath a magenta awning, she gripped the Java Stop's door handle. A miniature silver bell hung from the door hinges by a piece of ribbon, and the flat chime suddenly reminded her of the Kwik-Mart and mouthfuls of sweet ice.

A middle-aged woman waved to Erica from behind the maple countertop. "How are you doing?" She had scarlet coral beads woven into the ends of her auburn hair, and her slight neck was decorated with a pair of weathered hemp necklaces.

"Fine," Erica said, scanning the empty coffeehouse. The lone customer was a young boy sitting at the end of the counter. He had an outdated copy of *Better Homes and Gardens* propped on his stained knees, and he was plucking the subscription coupons from the magazine's spine and molding spontaneous origami.

"Can I get you something?"

"Just a Diet Coke." Erica found her wallet at the bottom of her purse and then checked her watch. She'd made it twelve hours without chewing a single thing, and she hadn't even pushed herself.

The woman placed a sixteen-ounce bottle on the countertop and then turned around to grab a ceramic coffee mug. "And you're sure nothing to eat?"

"I'm fine," Erica said coolly, staring at her own reflection in the mirror above the bar. She pulled a napkin from the dispenser and lightly dabbed her chin.

Erica walked to the back corner of the Java Stop and fell into a worn armchair. Unscrewing her Diet Coke, she emptied half of the soda into her mug. The fizzing carbonation rose to meet the lip of the mug like a tamed cloud.

Digging her hand into her jeans, Erica slid her cell phone onto her lap and stared at the blank screen. She'd stripped the battery off the faceplate after Ted's call, and she still couldn't decide if she wanted to check her messages. She brushed her forefinger against the power button and then shoved the phone back into her jeans.

Through the plateglass window of the Java Stop, Erica watched a pair of grade-school girls sharing a Tasti D•Lite on the sidewalk. She pictured the girls slumped in their chipped desk chairs, ignoring their algebra teacher, decorating their notepaper. Staring at the tight cones of their breasts, Erica saw the girls in front of their floor-to-ceiling mirrors delicately performing their daily measurements, wishing.

The doorbell sounded again. Doctor Rudas stepped confidently into the Java Stop in frayed khakis and a patched corduroy jacket. He smiled at Erica and trickled his fingertips through a practiced wave.

"Hey," Doctor Rudas began, sitting down in the opposing armchair. "You found the place all right?"

"Yeah."

"You seem to have calmed down a bit."

Erica smirked and spun the Diet Coke's plastic cap around the grooved bottle top. "I'm done with all of you people."

"All of us people?"

Erica nodded to herself. "All of you people in my life."

"Does it feel odd to be back in Manhattan—"

"Fuck the city," Erica muttered.

The young boy's creased brow emerged from behind *Better Homes and Gardens,* anxiously searching the coffeehouse. Doctor Rudas stretched his arm toward the counter and reassuringly patted the air. The boy ducked back behind the glossy cover.

"Did you make the list?" Erica asked.

"Yes, but I was hoping we could talk for a few minutes."

"What's on your mind these days?"

Doctor Rudas grinned. "I guess I've been thinking about our conversation last night, and a few things just aren't making sense to me. Maybe it was late."

The cashier arrived at their table with a mug of hot water, and Doctor Rudas cautiously selected a bag of Darjeeling.

Erica waited for the woman to retreat behind the counter. "Fire away."

"Well, first off, I don't understand why Ted told you. I mean, if he was working for your father, then . . ."

Erica crossed her legs and winced at the dull throbbing in her gut. "Are you saying you don't believe me?"

"No, I—"

"Then just give me the list, doc," Erica declared, clenching her teeth.

Sitting forward, Doctor Rudas gripped Erica's damp palm, cradling the dead weight of her fingers. "Okay." He flipped open a small spiral notebook, tore off the top sheet, and passed it to her. "The names are a little hokey, but . . ."

"Seascape House," Erica read. "New Beginnings, Walker-Lukes Center."

"I've written the addresses, Web sites, special features—"

"Seascape has DirecTV?" Erica asked.

Doctor Rudas shrugged. "Some people like that about—"

"And nobody knows you're there?"

"Not a soul," Doctor Rudas whispered into his steaming mug.

"So what are they going to make me do?"

"Think of it like a spa where there are things." Doctor Rudas paused. "Resources. Twelve-Step meetings. Group discussions. But you don't have to—"

"So I don't have to deal with doctors if I don't want to?"

"If you feel like spending a month in your room, you're free to."

"Or I could just walk out the door?"

"At the drop of a hat," Doctor Rudas said, swirling his tea bag and dropping it onto the saucer.

"I can just call a cab and—"

"Absolutely, one hundred percent guaranteed."

Erica dog-eared the corners of the sheet. "Are you going to charge my dad for this session?"

"No," Doctor Rudas said flatly. "This one's on the house. But I did want to mention the fact that each of these places is fairly pricey."

"I've got my own money."

"And, obviously, you'll want to find a discreet way to pay for it."

Erica swished a drink of soda. "What are you going to say when my father calls?"

"If he does, I'll simply tell him the truth."

"What's the truth?"

"That I don't know where you are."

Erica studied Doctor Rudas's shy grin. "You know there's no way I'd be doing this if Ted—"

"I know." Doctor Rudas jiggled his chin deliberately. "It's a rare synchronicity."

"And you don't care?"

"You know how they say the path to hell is paved with good intentions? Well, maybe the path to heaven is paved with bad ones."

Erica slipped the sheet of paper into the back pocket of her jeans. "I like that."

"I thought you might."

"So are we supposed to keep having our talks or whatever?"

"If you'd like, but I'm sure your father would notice if—"

"I'll pay for them," Erica interrupted.

Doctor Rudas sat back in his chair and furrowed his eyebrows. "Erica, that's quite a handsome compliment."

"I still think you're an asshole," Erica said, gazing out onto First Avenue.

"I wouldn't have it any other way," Doctor Rudas conceded.

"Good."

"I'll leave it to you to e-mail me, then. I mean, when you're settled."

"All three of these places are expecting me?" Erica asked.

"All three are expecting an eighteen-year-old female patient of mine."

"Right."

Doctor Rudas rested his mug on the table. "Well, I should probably get back to the apartment. My wife—"

"I think I'm just going to sit here for a bit."

"Take your time," Doctor Rudas said, standing up. He dropped a pair of singles on the table and buttoned his jacket. "They're all great places."

Erica nodded. "We'll see."

Date: Friday, 3 Oct 17:09:36
From: CharlesFIN@Highsmith.com
To: MichaelFIN@Highsmith.com

M—FUCK YOU. You're in no position to give me advice. You gummed this thing up from the beginning. I'm not paying another nickel.—C

Date: Friday, 3 Oct 17:21:56
From: MichaelFIN@Highsmith.com
To: CharlesFIN@Highsmith.com

That simply will not do. You chose the boy, not me. Furthermore, your daughter's condition is certainly not my fault.

```
Date: Friday, 3 Oct 17:54:20
From: CharlesFIN@Highsmith.com
To: MichaelFIN@Highsmith.com
```

M—This is the last email you'll ever get from me.
We're done.—C

The Lenox Hill Hospital security guard flipped open a Marlboro box top and snapped his Zippo against his suit pants. Ted checked the split-bars on the Jetta's dashboard clock. 6:04 P.M. Every thirty minutes, the security guard stepped through the hospital's sliding doors and burned through three-quarters of a cigarette.

Ted tilted the antenna of his cell phone toward the Jetta's sunroof, ushering the fourth bar of reception onto the screen. He shook the plastic casing and begged the mail icon to appear.

"One saved message. First saved message received at 5:22 P.M."

He listened to the choppy murmur of a crowd. The whip crack of a billiards break swept through the white noise.

"Ah, du du du dude, where are you? Du du du dude, where are you? Oh, Barbara Ann, where's my fucking car—"

James's gargled octave clicked off, and Ted flopped his chin onto the steering wheel. Down the block from the security guard, Ted watched an elderly Hispanic woman reorganizing a fresh-fruit stand with pyramids of glossy pears and softball grapefruits. She plucked an orange from the cardboard crates hidden underneath her tablecloth and tossed it to the security guard. The guard smoothly cradled the lob.

Ted pushed the driver's-side door open, and a young suit angrily sidestepped the door. "Watch it, pal," the suit yelled, thumbing his BlackBerry keyboard. "Fuck."

"Sorry." Ted folded his right leg back inside the car and slammed the door shut.

An Explorer veered out of the line of traffic, and a young Korean woman pointed at Ted's parking space. He shrugged. Her window glided down to half-mast, and she thrust insistently at the Jetta. "You leaving?" she barked.

"No," Ted shouted inside his sealed cabin.

The Korean woman glared back at Ted and then sped down Seventy-sixth Street.

Ted dropped his gaze to the stiffening Fish Filet on the dashboard. A pair of crescent bite marks smiled back at him. Two hours earlier, he'd swerved the Jetta into the cobblestone curb of Riverside Drive, pitched the door open, and emptied his guts all over 101st Street. He could still hear the wet sounds of stomach acid and French fries splattering against the asphalt.

Ted cleared his throat and felt the smoldering traces of bile warm his sinuses. Gripping his glass bottle of apple juice, he gargled the sweet water and let it slip past his tongue. He dropped the empty bottle into a cup holder and then picked up his phone and punched in ERICA CELL. The line droned through a long opening ring.

"What?" Erica answered.

"Erica?" Ted started.

"What do you want?"

Ted braced his elbows on the branches of the steering wheel and drew a couplet of quick breaths. "Are you okay?"

"Ted, you have to stop—"

"I just need to talk to you," Ted begged.

"I can't now," Erica said firmly. "I'm—"

"When?"

"I don't know. I've got to go."

"Okay," Ted whispered down to the floor mats.

"Bye." *Beep.*

Clutching his cell phone in a tight fist, Ted drove his hand into the Jetta's sunroof. "Fuck!" he yelled.

Across the street from the Jetta, the sloping grille and wide headlights of a Lincoln Town Car pulled into the red-striped No-Standing Zone. The Lincoln's strobing rear hazards pulsed above a pair of bumper decals, ELITE 329, and Ted watched the sidewalk reflections marbling over the tinted passenger windows.

Ted squeezed SEND again. The line tripped into Erica's staticky recording, and he waited for the sharp flute of her voice-mail box.

"Hey," Ted began. "I know you don't want to talk to me right now, but there are some things I need to say, okay? So just listen to this message. I mean even if you never want to talk to me again or anything. Just listen to me. Please."

The Lincoln's driver's-side door swung open, and a bulky Sikh in a wrinkled blazer climbed out and walked swiftly around the slick hood.

"You need to do me a favor. I mean you don't owe me a fucking thing ever, but I'm begging you. Just go to the e-mails. They set up this stupid fucking e-mail account for me, and everything's stored in that Inbox—www.Highsmith.com. Username: TedFIN. Password: York. It's all fucking there, and none of it mattered, okay?

"And I know it doesn't change anything," Ted panted. "And I know I sound ridiculous, but I don't fucking care, and I can't live with you thinking that I don't care about you. I can't ever make anything right, but I need to make it true, okay?" Ted stabbed END.

The Sikh arrived in front of the security guard, and the guard waved confidently at the sliding doors. Returning to the Lincoln, the Sikh crouched down and reported his findings to the shadowed line of the window slit. He stepped away from the car and pulled the back door open. A leather ankle-strap pump edged past the door frame, unveiling the gum ball of an ankle.

Ted hunched forward, squinting, as his tart breath wheezed out of his chest.

Erica stepped out of the Lincoln and carefully fastened the anchor buttons on her peacoat. Sweeping her hands through her hair, Erica nodded to the Sikh and nervously folded her lips against each other, marrying fresh coats of matte lipstick. On taut strides, she waded through the crisscrossing current of pedestrians.

Ted fell back against the driver's seat, trying to decipher how Erica had managed to age so gracefully in the handful of hours that she'd been away from him. It wasn't the formality of eye shadow or the sharp seam of dress slacks. Erica had shed the aimless gestures of dorm life and gotten dressed with money.

Date: Friday, 3 Oct 18:13:52
From: MichaelFIN@Highsmith.com
To: CharlesFIN@Highsmith.com

You hysterical little bitch, if you want messy, I'm more than happy to go messy. Finally, Erica should be arriving at your bedside in a matter of minutes and, you'll be happy to know, she looks fabulous, really fabulous. Are those Manolo Blahniks she's wearing?

The double-wide doors of the elevator slid open on the third-floor landing, and Erica stepped around two electricians in cloudy jumpsuits. A horseshoe reception desk presided over the floor's parallel hallways. Beyond the fuchsia wings of the desk, patient doorways stretched endlessly down the specked linoleum.

A wiry Irish nurse exited the glasshouse of the attendant station and smiled at Erica. "Visiting hours are over."

"I'm here to see my father," Erica said. "Reception said Charles Prakers was on this floor."

The nurse looked up from a cafeteria tray of miniature paper cups and studied the pastel bricks on her flat-screen monitor. "And you're his daughter?" she asked, tapping the keyboard's arrow keys.

"I have my driver's—"

"No worries," the nurse interrupted. "You've got his eyes."

"What about his fat ass?"

The nurse jerked her head to attention as the tail of Erica's grin dissolved from her lips. "You know his operation's at seven?"

"Well, then, we've got no time to waste," Erica began. "What room's he in?"

"Three-one-four." The nurse double-checked her screen. "Second to last on your right," she said, nodding over her shoulder. "Would you like me—"

"No, I'm fine. Thank you."

The walls of the corridor were plastered with a collage of children's watercolors, and Erica smiled stiffly at a construction-paper triptych of a giant pink fish with jagged teeth. Crossing through the spilled light of the third-to-last door frame, she carefully rehearsed her evening plans. Coffee with Laura at seven-thirty. Then straight to Modell's to buy a camping trunk. Erica reconsidered a second trunk and decided against it. Anything that wouldn't fit, she probably didn't need in the first place. One hour to pack and then a taxi to Penn Station.

Erica's heels slid noiselessly across the triangular tiles and turned into the doorway of room 314. The first thing she spotted was The Ferret, perched in a corner armchair, wearing a navy power suit and working through a delicately folded copy of *Quest* magazine. Erica hid against the metallic paint of the door frame and stared at the sheer glaze on her father's pedicured toenails. The whipstitched hem of a turquoise blanket shielded his calves and then rose sharply to cover his beach-ball belly.

"Oh, my!" Susan clutched the magazine to her blouse. "Thank heavens you're okay. Charles," she hissed impatiently.

Erica dodged Susan's air kiss. "How are you?"

"We were so worried when we couldn't reach you," Susan said, drawing the back of her hand across her temples. "We thought you were coming in this morning."

"Uh-huh." Erica nodded.

Charles's head lolled forward onto the pillow, and his left palm waved open-closed, open-closed, like he was testing the grip on a putter. "Hey, kiddo," Charles began. His legs and arms were strung to a cobweb of plastic sensors and monitors, and he suddenly reminded Erica of a retired marionette.

"You look rested," Erica said, forcing herself to make eye contact with her father. No matter what, she wanted him to remember her pride.

"They gave him some Valium," Susan added. "Just to calm him down beforehand and everything."

Erica studied her father's sleepy grin, trying to discern how much he already knew. In the end, she decided it didn't really matter.

Susan folded her arms across her chest. "I'm just so—"

"Can I talk to him?" Erica interrupted.

"Of course."

"Alone."

"Well, you—you—" Susan stuttered as she watched Charles

gently nod. "I'll just go grab the *Times*. Can't have enough to read," she said, tugging her coat off the brass coatrack.

Erica gripped the crown back of a hospital chair and slid it toward her father's bedside. Staring at his dazed, bloodshot eyes, she waited for her riot of accusations to settle.

"I know about Ted," Erica said.

A sour grimace broke the corners of Charles's lips, and he rolled his head away from Erica and onto the opposite side of the pillow. Reaching up to his thick bed of stubble, he scratched at the peak of his chin.

"Tell me why you did it," Erica declared, "or I swear I'm just going to walk the fuck out of here."

Charles gulped the astringent hospital air. "Erica, you're missing the forest for the trees."

"And what the hell does that mean?"

"It means . . ." Charles exhaled. "Fifty-thousand-foot overview, I helped a kid who needed helping."

"You bought a fucking spy," she cried.

"That's just not true," Charles said, shaking his head dismissively. "Do you even know York's story?"

"I know enough to—"

"Jim and Doug and the boosters fucking dropped him. A good kid pulls the short straw, and they say, 'Go pound sand.'"

"So you throw money—"

"And, yes, I probably said, 'Keep an eye out for my girl,' but that was it." Charles sliced his flat hand over his blanket. "I didn't even know if you guys would ever sync up."

"And so this is what," Erica begged, "Ted's paranoid fantasy?"

"Well," Charles began, and propped his broad chest on the crutch of his elbow. "It's pretty obvious somebody dropped the ball."

"Enough," Erica shouted, tipping her chair forward and

bounding away from her father toward the paneled windows. She pressed her fingers against the chilled double panes. "I didn't come here to listen to your fucking excuses."

Charles lay back against his pillows and corkscrewed his pinkie into his right ear. "Well, I'd hope," he said hesitantly, "I'd hope you just wanted to see me."

Erica bowed her head against the glass sheet. "I came to say good-bye, Dad."

"My odds aren't *that* bad," Charles grunted.

"Not that kind of good-bye," Erica said, cocking her chin.

"Erica." Charles sighed. "I'm sorry, okay? I should've told you everything right off the bat. I just didn't think you'd care. It was a fucking shave off my annual lot."

"Why can't you just admit it?" Erica asked, exhausted.

"Because you've blown this thing way out of proportion. You get fixated on things, and they take on a life of their own."

Erica squeezed the silk lining of her coat pockets into damp fists. "I guess it doesn't really matter," she said, spinning around to face her father.

"Erica—"

"Tomorrow I'm going to call school and ask for a leave of absence. I'll be out of this fucking country in under twenty-four hours. And I swear if you do one thing to try and stop me, I'll—"

"What the hell are you talking about?"

"If there's an absolute emergency, Laura will know how to contact me," she continued. "But I've told her to screen out any bullshit."

"You're smoking crack."

Erica shrugged. "I don't need your permission. It's one of the few perks of turning eighteen. That and voting."

Down the hall, the crisp tapping of heels punctured the air.

"And who," Charles said, nodding haughtily, "who do you expect to pay for your little adventure?"

Susan walked swiftly through the doorway, cradling the stacked sections of *The New York Times* and playfully miming the weight of her load. "They shouldn't be allowed to put any more coupons in," she joked.

"I woke Doug Gough up this morning," Erica explained. "In East Hampton—"

"What the fuck for?" Charles bellowed.

"To find out what was really mine, exclusively mine."

"Erica, Doug needs to be in his office to—"

"One-point-three," Erica finished. "That you can't fuck with no matter what."

Susan looked up from the Metro section and splayed the pages over her knee. "Language, guys," she whined, winking at Charles.

Charles whipped the top of the blanket off of his chest and exposed his shaved stomach. "You and I both know that's not what the money's for."

"Oh, I'm sorry. Am I supposed to use it to buy people instead? It's Mom's fucking money—"

"Hey, guys," Susan interrupted. "What's going on here?"

Erica spun around to meet Susan's plaintive grin. "This has nothing to do with you," she snapped.

"Your dad's dealing with a lot—"

"Erica's divorcing me," Charles said flatly.

"What?" Susan asked.

"It's a fucking carve-out," Charles declared.

On the bedside table, the cream push-button telephone whistled through its opening jangle. Susan rose promptly to her feet and stepped toward the phone.

Charles looked up at Erica. "So it's all a push?" he asked. "On your board, this cancels out everything else I've ever done, net-net."

Erica coiled a wisp of hair around her earlobe and watched Susan tuck the handset against her jacket's shoulder pad. "You know I don't think like you do," Erica said.

"Charles," Susan began. "A young man is downstairs, but reception says it's after hours."

"Fucking Wei. Tell him to leave the markup with the front desk."

"No, it's a Ted Cork," Susan said.

Erica's jaw snapped shut. The blades of her canines pierced a ripe slice of her lower lip.

"Erica," Charles pleaded. "It's—"

"Laura will call you." Erica shrouded her trembling frame in the cloak of her peacoat. "With her numbers."

Charles's fingers spread a broken veil over his eyes. "Erica," he begged. "I—"

"Enough," Erica yelled.

Susan stumbled backward, dropping the plastic handset against the frame of the hospital bed.

"I'm sorry," Charles mouthed.

Erica whirled around and walked quickly out into the hallway.

Date: Friday, 3 Oct 18:35:03
From: MichaelFIN@Highsmith.com
To: CharlesFIN@Highsmith.com

The silent treatment . . . How droll. If I don't hear back from you by the time I finish this wonderfully tepid Diet Pepsi, I might just have to break your world in two.

Ted traced his fingers around the brass numerals: 3, 1, 4. Rapping his knuckles against the door, he slipped back on his heels. A hollow voice filtered out to the hallway, and Ted hesitated and then gently opened the door.

Charles was sitting up on the edge of his bed. "What the fuck do you want?"

"Where's Erica?" Ted asked, staring at Susan.

Charles reached over to his nightstand and tugged a swatch of tissue paper. "She wrote me off." Lying back down on his cluster of pillows, he draped the diaphanous square over his face. "I'm not good with people, Ted." The tissue paper fluttered against his lips like a ship's pennant.

"Where's Erica?" Ted repeated, surprised by his sudden force-fulness.

"She left," Susan declared. "And this isn't—"

"Why the fuck are you here?" Charles interrupted.

"Sir." Ted lowered his head. "I guess I just want to tell you that I quit. I can't do—"

Charles ripped the tissue-paper mask from his face and glared at Ted. "Yeah," he said sarcastically. "Thanks for the fucking heads-up, kid."

"Damn you, Charles," Susan cried. She walked hurriedly around Charles's bed frame and stepped past Ted into the hallway.

"I mean, my stuff," Ted stammered, "should be out of the dorm by tomorrow night, probably."

Charles shook his head in disbelief and cleared his throat. "Finish the semester," he offered carelessly. "It doesn't fucking matter to me anymore."

"I don't want to. Sir—good-bye, sir," Ted said, starting for the door.

"Ted," Charles barked.

Gripping the cool metal of the doorknob, Ted caught his stride and spun back into the room.

"You told her?" Charles tugged on his earlobe. "I mean—"

"Yes, sir."

"You couldn't have just quit, walked away?" Charles asked. "I mean, without hurting her like this."

"Erica deserves better than us, Mr. Prakers."

"Even if that means throwing your own future away?"

Ted flexed his knuckles nervously against his hip. "She deserves better than us," he said softly.

Charles sighed and returned his gaze to the ceiling. "Who knows what we each deserve?"

"Good-bye—"

"Ted," Charles began, pursing his lips. "Did you fall in love with my daughter?"

"What?" Ted said, startled.

"Nothing else makes sense."

"I—" Ted hesitated as his eyes flitted around Charles's bedspread. He rested his forehead against the thick of the door. "I think so, I guess."

"And?" Charles's voice waffled. "Does she? I mean, do you think Erica loves you back?"

"I think she probably did care about me. Before—"

"Right." Charles tapped his thumbs together pensively. "You know, Michael's the smartest person I've ever met when it comes to people, their wants, their needs. But he doesn't get the simplest fucking thing of all."

Ted scratched at his Adam's apple. "I probably don't understand."

"If you do speak to her again," Charles said up to the plaster-board, "tell her I'd give everything I have to unwind this whole thing."

"I'm sorry, sir, but I can't."

"I understand," Charles conceded. "It'd be nice, though. If there was some way for her to know."

"I guess you're probably right."

Charles lifted his wrinkled palm off the mattress and flashed a wave. "Now get the fuck out of my sight. . . ."

"Good-bye, sir," Ted said, edging out of the room.

On Seventy-sixth Street, the setting sun was searing through an Atlantic fog cover and layering the sidewalk in a dank haze. Ted stepped in between ambulance bumpers and waited for the traffic signal. A Buick livery braked to a stop in front of him. The driver's four-finger ring tapped the crest of the wheel expectantly. Ted waved politely to the driver and shuffled across the asphalt.

Pressing the UNLOCK button, Ted lowered himself back into the Jetta's driver's seat and slid the serrated key into the ignition. He tugged the seat belt across his chest and swiveled the rearview mirror.

"You look terrible," Michael announced from the backseat.

"Fuck!" Ted leaped forward, frantically gripping the steering wheel.

Uncrossing his charcoal slacks, Michael leaned toward Ted and perched his chin atop the passenger seat. "Hi."

"How the fuck did you find me?"

"We just keep underestimating each other," Michael said, spiking his thin eyebrows.

Ted jerked around in his seat. "I—I'm useless to you."

Michael splayed his fingers defiantly. "Do you have any idea how much you've cost me?"

"But—"

"Dollars and cents."

"But I told her everything."

"Would you mind shutting the fuck up?" Michael shouted. Reaching underneath the pocket flap of his sport jacket, Michael slid out a stainless-steel gun and laid the pistol on his thigh. "Me, me, me, me," he sang.

Ted looked down at the buffed silver of the notched rear sight. "I—"

"Two hundred and twenty-five thousand dollars."

Falling back against the driver's seat, Ted wiped his palms on his jeans. "What . . ."

"Now, the way I figure it," Michael continued, "your family hovel would cash out at fifty grand on the sunniest of sunny days. And let's say, just for argument's sake, that you could squirrel away five thousand a year at Foot Locker."

"I don't care," Ted said softly.

"And let's say magnanimous Mom and princely Pop chip in another fiver."

"I don't care," Ted whispered to himself.

"So," Michael drawled, "we're looking at a seventeen-year payment plan. And that's assuming I'm in an interest-free kind of mood."

Ted turned back to Michael's cocksure grin, trying not to stare at the pistol. "Are you going to kill me?"

"No, Gimpy." Michael laughed. "That'd be far too painless. I rather like the idea of you living out the rest of your shitty life."

Ted nodded stiffly and twisted the car key. "Then get the fuck out of my ride."

"Your ride?" Michael cried. "We both know this is Debbie Redman's Jetta. And besides, we're going on a little errand together."

"What?"

"Consider this your act of absolution for—"

"Where?"

Michael raised his hitchhiker's thumb and waved it clumsily over his shoulder, through the rear windshield. "Well, to see your girlfriend, of course."

"I don't know where she is."

"Not to worry," Michael said. "She got home five minutes ago. Eight-twenty Fifth Avenue."

"How do you know she's there?"

"I'm the Wicked Witch of the East Side."

Ted slapped the rearview mirror, jerking the reflection onto Michael. "And what the fuck do you do when it rains?"

"That's the West." Michael slid his finger around the trigger. "Now drive the fucking car, Dorothy."

"Fuck you," Ted said, ripping his hands off the wheel. "I'm the one who screwed you. Erica—"

"Do you know Henry Moore?" Michael interrupted.

"My roommate's friend?"

"Close, but he was actually a twentieth-century English sculptor."

"I fucking care," Ted muttered.

"Well, obviously," Michael agreed. "But you see, you and I are going to go pick up a cute Henry Moore at the Prakers' place."

"You think I'm going to help you steal a sculpture?" Ted asked incredulously.

"Steal is far too dramatic, my friend. Far too moralistic—"

"You've lost your fucking mind."

"But, see, then I'll be square with Charles and Erica," Michael began, seesawing his head back and forth, "and you'll be square with me, Ted. I mean, all I'm asking you to do is simply carry the statue back to the car and then hand me the keys."

"You want to steal this car, too?" Ted laughed. "Fucking perfect."

"You stole it first," Michael said indignantly.

Ted raised his hands plaintively toward the sunroof. "And then it's over? Done? All of it? I never have to see you, hear from you, anything?"

"Well, don't dance around the issue, but yes."

Ted dragged his fingernails across the back of his neck. Down the block, he watched a young dog walker trailing his cat's cradle of nylon leads. Behind the pack of collies and retrievers, an eager FedEx deliveryman hopped from his elevated seat and padded underneath an awning. "I'll do it—"

"Splendid," Michael exclaimed.

"But I'll only do it alone," Ted said. "You stay in the car the entire time. If you take one—"

"Fabulous. More than fabulous," Michael cooed. "I'll tell you exactly where it is."

Ted spun around and met Michael's fevered gaze. "No bullshit."

Cupping the pistol in his right palm, Michael solemnly brought his hands together, sandwiching the steel body. "No bullshit. Now, head straight till you hit the park, then left."

Ted slapped the gearshift into DRIVE and wound the steering wheel into Seventy-sixth Street. Easing his sneaker onto the accelerator, he guided the Jetta out in front of a pair of taxis. "And what are you going to do when Charles calls the cops?" Ted asked as the front axle rocked past Park Avenue's manicured islands.

"It'd be a rather awkward police report. Don't you think?"

Ted hooked his fingers around the horn's stitched leather.

"You see, Mr. Officer, sir, I paid two gentlemen to spy on my daughter, and, well, when I ripped them off for hundreds of thousands of dollars, they took my new Henry Moore."

"Whatever." Ted braked for a red light on Madison Avenue. "It's going to be your fucking problem, not mine."

"That's a perfectly reasonable way of looking at things."

An M3 bus waddled through the intersection, and Ted stared

straight ahead at an elderly man semicircled by an audience of greedy pigeons.

"Can I ask you a personal question?" Michael said, stroking his finger along the barrel of the gun. "Man to man."

"What?"

"Someone in your shoes, a real salt-of-the-earth, Springsteen American. Were you afraid to improve your station in life?"

Ted's fingers strangled the gearshift as he listened to the anxious chorus of car horns behind him. "Go fuck yourself," he said. If he lunged over the armrest, Ted knew he could club Michael's jaw with the butt of his fist.

Michael's hoarse laughter filled the cabin. "Oh, Ted, you certainly can't keep blaming me for this bloody mess. It was always your choice, no?"

"I'll worry about my own side of the street," Ted declared, and flattened the accelerator. The Jetta leaped through the crosswalk and sailed toward Central Park.

"If Charles and I had had our way, you'd be studying for midterms presently and—"

"That's such fucking bullshit," Ted shouted. "That's—"

"Fine," Michael conceded, "but it was always your decision." He slouched down against the backseat, bristling the shoulder pads of his sport jacket. "I'm not a bad person, Ted. I just help people do bad things."

"Stop," Ted said. "Just stop."

Ted flicked the turn-signal wand and glided the Jetta onto Fifth Avenue. Oak trees anchored the park's cobblestone promenade. The horizontal slats of park benches hung together with charcoal bolt heads like treble clefs.

"If Erica won't let me in . . ." Ted eased his sneaker onto the brake pedal. "I mean if she won't even talk to me or anything, this whole fucking thing is off. I'll—"

"Let me worry about her," Michael offered. "I like to think I have a way with women."

"You're not getting out of this fucking car," Ted said, veering around a bike messenger.

Michael leaned forward and massaged Ted's shoulders. "Figure of speech," he corrected. "I meant only if she puts up a fight. But I can't see how she's going to care about her father now. She'll probably offer to gift wrap it for you."

Ted drove the pedal into the floor mat, and the Jetta lurched forward. "I swear if you take one step out of this car, I'm going to beat the living shit out of you."

"Blah, blah, blah," Michael groaned as he bounced back against the seat cushions. "I really don't think you're in any position to boss me around, Theodore."

Ted swerved the Jetta into the park-side lane. "I'm pulling over."

"And where would you like me to shoot you? In that bum leg or a good ol'-fashion' gut shot?"

Breezing past Fifth Avenue's flapping awnings, Ted gunned the engine and watched the speedometer curve past forty miles per hour.

"I'm a novice marksman," Michael mused, "but I can't imagine missing at this range."

"Maybe you're right," Ted said, gripping the waistband of his seat belt and pulling it taut.

Michael balanced his penny loafers on the hump of Ted's armrest. "Don't drive angry."

Bracing his hands at two and ten, Ted stared down the avenue's course of knotted oaks. "I guess I should apologize."

"Well," Michael said considerately, "we're making things right, Ted."

The Jetta sped through the Sixty-sixth Street crosswalk, and Ted eyed the raised lip of the curb. *"Spaldy,"* he whispered, *"be with me now."*

"What?" Michael started.

Gliding his hands together in a sculling grip, Ted yanked the steering wheel sharply to the right. The passenger-side wheels of the Jetta collided with the cement curb and ramped the front axle of the car into the evening air. Ted folded his arms across his chest; his eyes slid closed. Glass splinters burst out of the windshield as the hood of the Jetta dove forward and curled itself around the gnarled trunk of a silent oak.

Erica slouched down and rested her cheek against the purring vinyl of the seatback. The train's steady gallop was calming her stomach. Across the aisle, a young mother was cradling a portable DVD player for her son. A purple dinosaur waddled across the flat screen and projected kaleidoscopic hues onto the child's T-shirt.

Erica unwrapped her pack of prepaid postcards and plucked a ballpoint pen from her purse.

dear maisy, you're probably wondering where the hell i am. sorry about that. i wanted to let you know that i'm not coming back to school. a bunch of family stuff has come up and i have to deal with it now. i know this sounds crazy but it's what i need to do. anyway i wanted to ask you a favor since i don't really know who else to ask. will you clean out my side of the room? you can keep anything you want but i was hoping my clothes could go to the salvation army or goodwill and my books could just go to the library. i know debbie's laptop broke last week so maybe you could give her mine. sorry to drop all this on you. if you just want to dump everything in a

trash bag i guess i'd understand that too. good luck
with school and gymnastics and life. best, erica

Erica dropped the pen at her side. Waving the postcard dry, she
watched the disk-harrowed tracts glide by her window frame.
Beyond the fields and stalks of bent rushes, rows of highway brake
lights blurred into crimson starlets.

She reached into her purse and plugged her iPod's earbuds into
her ears. Flipping through Fiona Apple's track list, she hummed
the opening bars of "Shadowboxer." Wherever she was, Erica
decided, Fiona was always there to back her up.

She folded Maisy's card into the back pocket of her pants. She
picked a fresh postcard off the top of the pack and spotted the
corners with blueberry specks.

doctor r, i'm going to watch some directv. thought you'd
want to know. i stared my father down tonight and told
him goodbye. he threw a fit but he didn't say no. he
couldn't. and then i walked off the set of my life. i can't
really believe it but everything i own is sitting in a 3' by 2'
trunk. i don't even own a set of keys. no books. no jewelry
or makeup. no computer or cell phone. for the first time in
my life i only own one pair of shoes. if i got off this train
at some random town and checked into some random motel
that would be my home. being nobody feels pretty good.

Erica pinched another blank card from her purse.

card two. read this second. anyway i'm not making any
promises about how much directv i can watch. i'm going

to check out all the different channels for a couple days but i don't know if i'll subscribe to any of them. my only promise is that i'll listen to the broadcast and see if i'm supposed to hang around. to be honest i think i'm supposed to be on the other side of the atlantic right now. this trunk is begging to be covered in airport stickers. sincerely, guess who

Erica added the postcards to her pants pocket and adjusted the headrest. Her back muscles felt like the stretched cords of a hammock. Peering over the tops of the seats, Erica searched the aisle for directions to the snack car and then gave up. She didn't feel like wrestling with a menu. Besides, she reminded herself, it would be easier to fall asleep numb.

Miming her signature on her kneecap, Erica remembered tracing her fingers along the notched metal of Ted's thigh. She jabbed her nails into the armrest's grooved rubber and then lifted the last postcard from her purse.

ted, i can't decide if i should even write this postcard but there are some things i need to say to you. i can't ever forgive you for what you did to me but i don't blame you for my father. he used you. he uses everybody. my father controls people/things/life with money because that's all he knows. anyway i haven't read the emails you talked about and i'm not sure i'm going to. this is the most painful thing that's ever happened to me and i'm not going to relive it. it all needs to be over forever. so this is goodbye. i hope we're both happier wherever we are. p-fwast
p.s. i know you cared about me

An icy shiver twisted through Ted's legs and crinkled the crepe examination paper. He squinted up at a pair of ivory flying saucers, their halogen landing beams dropping directly onto his V-neck. Tracing the saucers' suspension arms up to the ceiling panels, Ted raised his right hand and searched for his forehead. There was nothing there. His fingers bumped against a sponged wall and recoiled.

A middle-aged Indian man stared down into his lazy pupils, and Ted immediately recognized his seashell lab coat and laminated badge. Ted watched the doctor's hands kneading the air in front of his belt buckle, tying invisible ribbons.

"The anesthetic is still wearing off," a woman's voice explained. "You may feel a little numb."

Rolling his head onto the other half of the pillow, Ted searched drowsily for the voice's body. A woman in a cyan polyester suit was sitting on the windowsill, smiling sincerely. Beyond the windowpanes, Ted could see the conical spotlights of city streetlamps.

"Where?" Ted said hoarsely.

The doctor danced his fingers above Ted's stomach.

"'You're in Lenox Hill Hospital,'" the woman continued flatly. "'My name is Doctor Parekh, and I am your attending physician.'"

Ted's eyes flickered between their calm gazes. A warm swell thawed his toes.

"'You were in a very bad car accident,'" the woman said as Doctor Parekh knocked his fists together. "'We've spoken to your parents, and they're going to be here in the morning.'"

"What time is it?"

"It's nearly ten in the evening."

Ted twisted back toward Doctor Parekh. "Why doesn't he—"

"'I'm deaf,'" the woman explained.

Doctor Parekh stroked his palm, and then his right index finger drew a rectangle around his lips.

"'And I can read your lips,'" the woman said. "'And then communicate with you using my interpreter and nurse, Molly.'" Molly thrust her erect thumbs at her jacket lapels. "'You should know that you have a grade-three concussion, and we're going to run a CT scan.'"

Ted surveyed the gurney station. Two starched teal curtains hung from metal rings and formed the third and fourth wall of his rectangle.

"'You're very lucky. The air bags saved your life.'"

"Where's Erica?"

"'Who?'" Molly translated.

"Nothing," Ted muttered.

Doctor Parekh's fingers somersaulted through a collection of poses and then pulled away from his body in tight fists.

"'You're going to heal very quickly,'" Molly read. "'You're young and healthy.'"

"What about Michael?" Ted asked.

"'Who?'"

"The other guy in the car."

Doctor Parekh framed an uppercase *L* with his right hand and rotated it against the face of his left hand.

"'Later. The important thing now is for you to rest up.'"

The hospital intercom popped with shrill feedback. "Code Orange in transit. Code Orange in transit."

Molly mimed a pistol with her right hand and wiggled the trigger.

"What?" Ted asked, watching Doctor Parekh decoding.

"Gunshot," Molly explained, and raced through a procession of gestures.

Nodding furiously, Doctor Parekh pointed at the break in the curtains.

"We'll be back," Molly said. She stepped quickly around Ted's gurney and followed Doctor Parekh through the billowing slit.

Electronic chimes echoed through the emergency room, mimicking heart rates and blood pressures. Rubber footsteps cheeped down the hallway.

"Who's on airway?" a doctor shouted. "Who's got circulation?"

"On it."

Ted stared at the downy curtains and pictured a crowd of milling lab coats and scrunched brows. The *click-clacking* of the metal trays and stainless-steel instruments hovered above their chatter, scoring Ted's memory stills. Whipped air. Mottled stones and tree pits. The front bumper exploding into iridescent metal sparks as adrenaline surged through the steering column and frosted his forearms. Blurred human dyes.

"Ted?" a voice carried over the curtains.

"Yeah," Ted whispered breathlessly.

"Bro," James said. "What's up?"

"Where are you?"

"Where the fuck are *you*?" James whined, and bloused the curtain at the foot of Ted's gurney. James was dressed in the navy sweater and starched chinos that he always wore to Sigma Chi dinners.

"Hey," Ted said as he watched James's grin fade.

"Hey," James repeated. "How you doing, man?"

Ted stretched his stiff jaw and shrugged.

James nodded anxiously. "Okay, okay." He rolled a leather wheelchair up to the gurney's metal braces, dropped the rubberized foot plates, and folded himself into the seat. "They said you were awake, so I thought I'd swing by and just, you know, swing by."

"Thanks." Ted tensed his bruised abdomen and pulled himself into a crunch. Reaching forward, he quickly untied his sneakers and knocked them off the edge of the gurney.

"Your 'rents called me," James continued. "And I figured I'd jump on an Amtrak. Especially while they're flying in and whatnot."

"Were they pissed?"

"Bro," James gasped. "We're all just pumped you're going to be okay."

"You think so?"

"Man, it's a fucking miracle." James hesitated and then leaned forward and squeezed the heel of Ted's right foot. "A fucking miracle, kid."

Ted forced a smile. "Is Michael here?"

"I'm not sure, but—"

"James," Ted interrupted, studying the ink dots of his blue eyes. "I need—"

"Dude, they're still working on him, but I bet he's going to pull through, okay?"

Ted's rib cage tightened and shrank his breath. "I'm going to jail, James."

"Ted, nothing's anybody's fault. Don't think that way."

"I'm not sure."

James rested his arms along the gurney's guardrail. "Well, you should know everybody in the dorm's really pulling for you, buddy."

"Thanks."

"You want me to run to the bookstore or whatever and pick up some magazines or something?"

"No, I'm fine." Ted tore a strip of examination paper off the gurney and gently dabbed his forehead. The cool jelly burned his eyebrows, leaving fossilized streaks of blood suspended against his skin. "I'm sorry about your car and everything."

James winced. "Don't worry about it. My dad's on his way to pick it up right now."

"How'd you find it?"

"Erica left me a voice mail. When I was on the train."

Ted nodded, smiling to himself. "Good."

"So you want me to keep hanging out here?" James asked.

"Yeah, I wouldn't mind."

"Cool, cool. Hospitals are filled with people and shit, but they're kind of lonely."

"Yeah," Ted agreed.

"Except for delivery rooms. Babies are cool."

"They are."

"But everything else kind of sucks," James said.

"It does."

 **NOVEMBER**

Date: Sunday, 2 Nov 15:34:09
From: CharlesFIN@Highsmith.com
To: TedFIN@Highsmith.com

Ted—I tried you at your school email address but I
haven't heard back. I hope this reaches you and
that you have a few minutes to write me. I wanted
to let you know that Michael and I have finally
agreed on a financial settlement. I don't know how
it all came to this but I'm just glad you're both
okay now. Also I sent Debbie Redman a check for a
new Volkswagen Jetta. It was the least I could do
after everything that's happened.—Charles

Date: Tuesday, 4 Nov 07:28:32
From: CharlesFIN@Highsmith.com
To: TedFIN@Highsmith.com

Ted—I'm planning to send a check to the university for your second-semester tuition. No strings attached. I promise. I hope this comes as good news. Again I'd really like to hear how you're doing.—Charles

----

Date: Friday, 7 Nov 09:49:16
From: CharlesFIN@Highsmith.com
To: TedFIN@Highsmith.com

Ted—I hope you don't mind but I called your dorm today and spoke with James. He said I should try you at your house in Illinois. I'm not going to do that. You know how to reach me if you want to. Good luck. I'm sorry about everything.—Charles

P.S. I mailed your second-semester payment this morning.

Erica traced the asphalt's split line down to the corner of Lasker and Silkworm, re-counting the white dashes. Twenty-two. Sitting forward on the porch steps, she rested her elbows on her knees and went back to studying the cosmos of insects flittering around the neighbors' floodlights.

Erica tucked her pink hospital bracelet underneath the cuff of her sweater. The secretary at Seascape House had offered to cut the plastic tag off yesterday morning, but she'd asked her to leave it on. Erica had gotten used to the feel of the bracelet and decided it was the perfect souvenir.

A Subaru wagon pulled onto Lasker, and Erica watched as the headlights glazed rows of lawns. The car braked to a stop on the far side of the street. She heard the whining metal of a door swinging open.

Cupping her hands around her eyes, Erica spotted the black-and-white jersey of a referee. The zebra stripes floated above the roof of the wagon, and she suddenly recognized the lethargic shrug of Ted's shoulders. He waved good-bye to the shaded cabin. The Subaru pulled away from the curb, and Ted strode unevenly across the asphalt.

Erica started to stand up and then tipped back onto the top step of Ted's porch. "Hey," she called out.

Ted snapped his head upright; his sneakers skidded across his gravel driveway. "Hey," he said, regaining his balance. Paul's parting demand had been a one-page essay on the 2nd Step and the word *sanity*, and Ted was busy crafting his first sentence.

"Sorry," Erica began.

"I . . ." He folded his arms around his Foot Locker jersey. "I didn't see you."

"I know."

Stepping carefully across his lawn, Ted sat down on the bottom step of his porch and gripped the wrought-iron banister.

"I tried knocking," Erica said, wishing he'd sat down next to her. "But nobody—"

"My folks are at work," Ted interrupted, staring at the roadway.

"Right."

Ted looked up at Erica and nervously fingered the belt loops on his black slacks. "I didn't think I was going to see you again."

"I know," she said. "So you got my postcard?"

"Sort of. James read it to me. Over the phone," Ted finished.

Erica scooted forward and lowered herself onto the bottom step of the porch. A blackberry bruise squirmed along Ted's temple, and it suddenly reminded her of a lost millipede.

"I didn't go back to school," Ted said. "I mean, I haven't been back."

"Me neither."

"My dad drove there a few weeks ago and packed up my stuff."

"Yeah," Erica said. "Maisy told me."

Ted arched his eyebrows. "When did you talk to her?"

"A couple days ago."

"Did she tell you?"

"Yeah," Erica said quietly.

Unfastening his tongue from the roof of his mouth, Ted felt his jaw stall. "Yeah," he repeated.

Erica sat back against the porch steps, waiting for her words to gather. Down the block, the roar of a televised laugh track washed over the chanting crickets. "You meant to crash it, right?"

"What makes you think that?"

"What are the odds of the same accident happening to the same person?"

Ted's thumbs twitched against the splintered edges of their wooden plank.

"Were you trying to . . . ?" she asked hesitantly. "Or—"

"I don't know what I was trying to do."

Erica nodded softly. "I'm so sorry, Ted."

"I'm sorry, too," Ted breathed.

"What did the police say?"

"Your father told them some story. I don't know. Something about Michael being his personal assistant. You knew me through school or something."

"Right."

Ted picked a dried dogwood leaf off the ground and crumpled the arrowhead into a dusty powder.

"How long were you in the hospital?" Erica asked.

"Forty-eight hours maybe," he said, sprinkling the cracked leaf onto the grass. "They couldn't believe how fine I was."

Erica rested her hand on Ted's leg and squeezed his thigh. "Do you want to go inside?"

"Do you want to come inside?" Ted asked, smiling uneasily.

"Ted—"

"Where'd you go?" he blurted out. "I mean, where have you been?"

"You're not going to believe it," Erica said, shaking her head.

"I think I'd believe just about anything right now."

Erica slipped her pink bracelet out from behind her sleeve. "I checked myself into a rehab."

Ted gazed suspiciously at the plastic band and then leaned forward and read the lettering: SEASCAPE HOUSE. "We admitted we were powerless over alcohol—that our lives had become unmanageable," he said, reciting the 1st Step from memory.

"Over food," Erica corrected. "But it's basically the same ideas."

"Right. Then I guess I'm supposed to say 'Welcome.'"

"I guess."

Tilting his head back, Ted scratched at his stubbly sideburns. "Did you like it? I mean, was it helpful?"

"It was amazing," Erica said, relieved. "I met some of the most amazing people in my life. Real people. The kind you just know are going to be with you forever."

"I'm glad."

"Are you doing the not-drinking thing or . . . ?"

"Yeah."

Erica spun the bracelet around her wrist and felt the tacky grip snagging wisps of her arm hair. "How long have you been sober now?"

Ted smirked and checked his Casio. "Since I got up this morning at eight A.M."

"I meant how many days?"

"I know," he said. "Thirty-five days."

"You're not going to believe this, but I love going to meetings now."

Ted nodded. "I knew you would."

"Ted—"

"Why are you here?" he asked, frightened by the fragile sound of his voice.

"Are you angry?"

"No," Ted exclaimed. "It's just that I convinced myself. I mean, I convinced myself that it was over. That we were finished, you know?"

Erica watched Ted's eyes darting around his front lawn. "I understand."

"And I'm terrified. . . . I mean, I'm terrified."

"Of what?"

"Everything, okay?" Ted declared. "I—"

"Okay."

Ted clamped his teeth together and felt the pinch needling his sinuses. "I can't stand you hating me again," he said, carefully pronouncing each syllable.

"I don't hate you, Ted."

"Why not?"

"I miss you."

Ted wiped his forehead with a tight fist. "I miss you, too."

"Do you believe me?"

"I don't know what—"

"Believe me," Erica pleaded, wishing she could cup his chin between her fingers.

Ted's lips curled into an exhausted frown. "I hate myself for it, Erica."

"But maybe it's not about the past," she said, sliding her sneaker across the grass and playfully nudging the sole of Ted's Nike.

"What do you mean by that?"

"I mean, I've spent the last month just thinking everything through. And maybe it's not about what you've been to somebody, but what you could be," Erica explained. "In the future."

"What could I really be to you?" Ted said down at their matching shoelaces.

Erica reached across the step and gently gripped Ted's shoulder. "A friend."

"A friend?" Ted asked curiously.

"A good friend."

"But just a good friend?"

Pinching the arch of Ted's neck, Erica closed her eyes and pressed their lips together. Ted's back stiffened. She felt him falling away from her. As she slipped forward, a chilled gust burned her lungs. Before she could open her eyes, Ted's palm caught her chin. His warm tongue tickled the roof of her mouth and replaced the numb tingling in her fingertips.

"A great friend," Erica exhaled, scattering kisses around his mouth.

Ted ducked into the crook of her neck and smoothed the strands of her hair against her skin.

"Do you believe me now?" she asked, cradling his head.

"I'm so sorry, Erica," Ted whispered.

"I know."

"I'm so—"

"It's okay."

Ted lifted himself up a step and wrapped his arms around Erica. Bear-hugging her against his chest, he felt her run kisses along his forearm. "So what do we do now?"

"Toss a dart into a map," Erica said, grinning. "Spain, Ireland, Australia."

Ted laughed and nuzzled his face in her curls. "You still like that idea?"

"I don't know. I don't really have a lot of plans these days."

"Well," Ted said, cupping her waist, "this town is perfect for laying low."

"Yeah?" Erica asked. "What do people do around here?"

"Lots of stuff, I guess. There's the mall." Ted tugged on the polyester collar of his jersey. "I mean it sucks, but . . ."

Erica looked up at Ted's nervous smile and tickled his neck. "I'm a city girl, Ted. I need action, noise."

"Stuff happens here."

"I don't know," she teased.

"Stuff will happen."

"What?"

Ted spotted kisses along the back of her hand. "Just wait. It'll happen."

"What if we miss it?"

"Just wait."